PRAISE FOR GAIL JONES

'Gail Jones has to be one of Australia's most consistently impressive writers. Her prose is evocative, her plots meaningful and her characters drawn with considerable care.'
Guardian

'One of Australia's most distinguished and highly awarded writers.'
Saturday Paper

'One of the most important and prolific literary authors working in Australia today.'
Sydney Review of Books

ALSO BY GAIL JONES

One Another

Salonika Burning

Our Shadows

The Death of Noah Glass

A Guide to Berlin

Five Bells

Sorry

Dreams of Speaking

Sixty Lights

Black Mirror

Fetish Lives

The House of Breathing

Gail Jones is the author of two short-story collections and eleven novels. Her work has been translated into several languages and has received numerous literary awards. Originally from Western Australia, she now lives in Sydney.

THE NAME OF THE SISTER

GAIL JONES

TEXT PUBLISHING MELBOURNE AUSTRALIA

The Text Publishing Company acknowledges the Traditional Owners of the country on which we work, the Wurundjeri people of the Kulin Nation, and pays respect to their Elders past and present.

textpublishing.com.au

The Text Publishing Company
Wurundjeri Country, Level 6, Royal Bank Chambers, 287 Collins Street,
Melbourne Victoria 3000 Australia

Published by The Text Publishing Company, 2025

Cover art and design by W. H. Chong
Page design by Rachel Aitken
Typeset in Granjon LT Std 13/18.5pt by J&M Typesetting

Printed and bound in Australia by Griffin Press, a member of the Opus Group. The Opus Group is ISO/NZS 14001:2004 Environmental Management System certified.

ISBN: 9781923058538 (paperback)
ISBN: 9781923059320 (ebook)

A catalogue record for this book is available from the National Library of Australia.

EU Authorised Representative: Easy Access System Europe—Mustamäe tee 50, 10621 Tallinn, Estonia, gpsr.requests@easproject.com

The paper this book is printed on is certified against the Forest Stewardship Council® Standards. Griffin Press, a member of the Opus Group, holds chain of custody certification SCS-COC-001185. FSC® promotes environmentally responsible, socially beneficial and economically viable management of the world's forests.

you are not alone,
the poem said,
in the dark tunnel.

Louise Glück, 'October'

I

Mostly he stared ahead. Or hid his face with his hands, oblivious.

Here was a white-haired man, sitting beside a crumpled house, blankly reporting that his wife and children were entombed. His head was low. His posture was huddled. Deprived of biography and interior, viewers saw only a pitiable surface, eyes pouched with weeping, skin ashen with knowledge of death, the faintest tremble of his hand raised in a shield to say, *Go away*.

It flew to the camera lens, faster than a speeding bullet.

It was the fleeting fame of innocents, alight in their distress, their faces caught in the extremity that commanded her interest.

And now it was snowing. Now what was lovely in the air was an extra torment, and in the flurry of emergency workers, or soldiers, or those just hanging about, there was no time to see more of this struggling man, who might hope, more than anything, to freeze to death, to stay here where he belonged, near the crushed bodies of his family, and beneath the softer, kinder collapse of not-yet-dirty snow.

Angie did not catch the name of the country in which this man was waiting for his own death. Already his face was gone, replaced by an aerial view. Already he was a token and a generalisation. The close-ups had been violating but no one cared. It was convention to make this misery spectacular and Angie had seen it so often now that she barely noticed. She used to weep over the evening news, watching the funerals of war victims, the pleas of widows, the long shots of blurrily pixelated corpses.

The next news item was different. It was not of catastrophe or war. It was a single woman, an amnesiac, and filmed in Sydney. On the television her face was narrow, brown in unnatural light and unearthly in appearance. There was a dismal tone to the report, and a banner at the bottom of the screen said *Unknown Woman: Information Wanted*. She did not know who she was. No one knew who she was. No one knew where she had come from. She had simply arrived. Her life was a puzzle waiting to be solved, so she carried the enticing air of one considered mysterious.

Although she seemed youngish—no more than forty—the woman sat in a wheelchair, her body at a tilt. She looked dazzled by the lights upon her, and her empty blink recalled the clicking eyelids of old-fashioned dolls. She was in a pea-green hospital gown, the sort with ties at the back; if her mystery had not been announced, you might suppose she was an addict, or a drunk, or some unfortunate, ordinary woman, harried by depression. But the commentary was emphatic: this was an Unknown Woman. She was unable to speak and could not give an account of herself.

A sombre doctor stood nearby, performing the role of guard, his hands folded at his crotch with the stern authority of duty, while a policewoman with a tight bun, impeccably neat, asked the public for assistance.

'Someone must know who she is,' she said. 'Someone out there. We've decided to call her Jane for now. We ask anyone with information to come forward, or to ring Crime Stoppers on the number on the screen.'

Why had the police subjected her in this way to the cruel devotion of the camera? Why not just show her photograph? The woman was touching her neck, as if seeking her own pulse. There was a refocus to follow this slightest of gestures.

The policewoman said that Jane was found wandering at night on a highway, thirty or so kilometres north-east of Broken Hill. She might have been the victim of a crime; they needed an identification.

The report swung to the man who had discovered Jane on the road. Before the camera he looked both lost and pleased with himself. The microphone was a black bulb beneath his furry chin. Middle-aged, a belly roll over the top of his shorts, a misshapen T-shirt (Def Leppard—old rocker) hanging stretched and loose. He had not dressed for an interview.

'Bit of a shock,' he grinned. 'Yeah, bit of a — shock.' A word had been bleeped out; the man had said 'fucking shock'.

Now, by some dark magic, Angie more fully imagined her. She was wavering in the headlights, a figure in a ragged dress, her feet bloody, perhaps, and her frame slowly staggering. This driver charging at the darkness saw a shape ahead and thought first of an animal. Knowing how to drive in the country, he slowed rather than swerved. And then the woman drifted towards him, a set of human angles and skinny as a new lamb, and he stamped his brake in panic, coming to a skidding halt—too close, too close (how his heart hammered).

He leaned over the steering wheel, muttering, 'What the fuck, what the fuck?' Instinctively, he reached to the passenger seat for his phone. His impulse was to stay still and make a call. He watched the woman sway in her own bright-lit isolation, stumble in small steps towards the headlight glare, then veer sideways in a clumsy jerk, as if she was coming to yank at the door of the car. But near the door she toppled; she was suddenly gone. She was there, then not, and only then the driver calmed a little and thought of rousing to help her.

'Fuck, fuck, fuck,' he declared aloud, as if the rat-tat-tat of fuck-fuck-fuck covered all and every confusion. Then he left the car, pressed his phone light on and held it up to search for the woman—and yes, he hadn't imagined it, there was a prone body in the ditch before him, fallen and very still. Only now he called Emergency.

The ambulance had miles to come, and a voice said, 'Don't

leave her, stay there, we're coming fast as we can,' and he was obliged in a way that made him feel schoolboyish and small. Again he burbled, 'Fuck,' as he stood at a distance, deciding. Eventually, he slid down to her, grazing his right elbow and hand on the way, and now he thought of a dead body, not of a woman.

Oh, but she groaned, and he flinched and leaned away, and so began the mystery of the Unknown Woman.

Urgently, he was speaking into his phone, 'What happens now?' and he was told to roll the woman onto her side, head slightly raised. 'Check her airways for obstructions,' the voice said. 'And cover her with something warm.' He didn't know what obstructions meant. He was afraid to touch her, so didn't.

He climbed back to his Ford Falcon, which was ticking and steaming, a tough-as-guts beast in the chilly desert night—such a beautiful vision, with its headlights flowing in the dark. He loved this car, and now it seemed more solidly alive than both of them. He fetched the old blanket that covered the spare tyre in the boot, shook it out a little, climbed down to the body and draped it over the woman without touching.

Now he felt competent; he might be saving a life. 'Done,' he said proudly.

'Wait there. Monitor her breathing, keep her warm.'

All this, this recreation, came from the faces on the screen, the man saying 'fucking shock'. Angie knew nothing of the case. But she saw how little protection there was for the woman in so rude an exposure. Somehow she guessed from the start that in the scene of discovered ravage, in the story of the road and the speeding car, in the tense panic of a near-miss collision and in the hulk of a Ford Falcon, fixing its steady headlights on a wonky woman, there existed an entire logic of what is concealed and unconcealed.

Angie carefully placed her glass of wine on the coffee table. Her husband, Sam, moved behind her and his large hand came to rest on her shoulder. Sam said nothing, sighed, then moved back to the preparation of their evening meal. Miniature, busy sounds, chopping and scraping. A reflection showed Angie outside, seated in her armchair on the tiles of their small courtyard. She was glossy in timeless night, and darkly transparent. It was an illusion she enjoyed. Herself in two places, her body pale and floaty, mislaid and contrapuntal, being its own ghost. Then the televisual scenes were gone in a flick, and the world comfortably contracted to the business of dinner.

On the night of the announcement, the news had not seemed a big deal and Angie had not yet decided she would research a story about Jane. The idea had not declared itself. Bright as Jane was in her mind, and the image of her standing before the car, it was the bereaved man, the snow man, she thought of later that night. Seen only for seconds, he persisted as a troubling shape.

And as she failed to fall asleep, it was the snow man's face that she saw, freezing and fading, willing subtraction, and in his dark eyes an annihilating sorrow.

After the first reports came a whirl of speculation. Social media went wild with Jane memes and Jane theories, and teams of shouty 'Janeites'. Jane's face was in the papers and on every television channel. Overnight, she became familiar and existed in further incarnations: digital images showed how she might have appeared at twenty, and at ten. What looked like a mugshot morphed in reversal and turned three hundred and sixty degrees. It was streaked with numbers and green lines, so that Jane emerged in deathly versions, staring into space. Angie was reminded of photographs in passports and ID cards, in which we see ourselves as we hope never to have been, pallid with the texture of candlewax, subdued, unbreathing, stuck fast in the little prison of a shiny square. The uncanny valley of our singular faces. How they pre-empt us.

The media interest brought no clarification, but it did enlist multitudes who claimed definite knowledge. Into hashtags and vox pops poured claims and proclamations. Scatty energies, rumours, dubious TV. Jane was the urban brick wall that begs to be tagged or sprayed.

Angie heard later that hundreds of people rang Crime Stoppers to say that they knew her, dead cert, for sure, one hundred and one per cent; she was a daughter, a lover, a runaway wife; she was the sister abducted from a playground at the age of nine; she was the teenage cousin who ran off with a stockman, on a whim or a spree, and was never seen again.

Someone recognised in Jane their personal trainer from five years ago. Another as the woman who sold drugs at Fairfield Station. A man rang from Tasmania to say that Jane was once his teacher; he never forgot a face and had been taught twenty years before by this still recognisable woman, who was 'fatter then, and blonde, but otherwise exactly the same'.

Angie had not known there were so many lost women out there, or that 'Unknown' was such an unbearable provocation. One talkback radio announcer, honey-voiced and compelling, had a genius for stirring up the past, and invited listeners to ring in with theories and scandals. Angie tuned in. She expected ww and publicity hounds, but was surprised how tender many of the stories were, how there was a fond, cherished aspect to even the thinnest fantasy or recollection, and that now, on the basis of Jane's publicly vulnerable face, they might love her again, or greet her again, or renouncing long years of resentment and antipathy, ask forgiveness or even forgive.

There were voices, pleading a case, some imagining Jane might be listening.

'Hello, Mary. Your mum and me are waiting at home. We know you're sorry and we are really, really sorry too. We shouldn't have said what we did...We really shouldn't have... Sorry, love.'

The policewoman, Detective Inspector Beverly Calder, was known to Angie, as they say in the trade. Journalists like to have a few police contacts, but the two women shared the dearest of friendships. Bev and Angie had been in the same class for their seven years of primary school. In their small town in the bush it was impossible not to know the others; the perpetual cohort made them inevitably connected.

Bev's father was the local cop, top-of-the-pile in a country town; Angie's was a jobbing labourer, fencing, tending sheep, drinking too much, sad. When she learned the word *feckless*, she thought first of him: her father was feckless. In town, status was linked to the role of the father (mothers, it seemed, didn't count at all), and a man in a uniform, even if it was only a khaki shirt and a wedged felt hat, was more important than a grubby bloke in a singlet who chopped other people's wood, who hung around embarrassing everyone when he was unemployed, and who had to be fetched from the pub, smelling of vomit, when his despair got the better of him. Angie's father had the glum notoriety of a failure. His wife and daughter were ashamed but loved him just the same, and it was difficult to bear.

When Angie rang, Bev said, 'Piss off—my case, not your story,' but they met for a drink after work and Bev could not resist disclosure. '"Fatter then, and blonde, but otherwise exactly the same"!' Bev laughed her donkey laugh, throwing back her head, snorting, full of cheeky amusement. Now that her hair was released from its bun, Angie saw a terrible perm.

'"Exactly the same"! That's what the caller said.'

Out of uniform, Bev recovered a more open self, unguarded and sometimes indiscreet, and Angie saw again how, for all their divergences, there was still the claim on each of them of a scratchy paddock or a hidden cubby, or a dusty, dim bedroom in which both had confided their desires. Often they had spoken in funny accents of no known country, asserting disconnection from their boring lives. Bev wanted desperately to learn the piano, but never would, not in a country town with no pianos or piano teacher. Angie wanted to travel to Egypt, where there was another history entirely, and pyramids, and women in murmurous robes who drew charcoal lines around their eyes. The girls lay side by side holding hands, chewing grass and staring up at a sulphur sky, and Bev said she would do a concert in Egypt one day, on a huge black piano, a grand piano, its lid open like the wing of a giant crow, and that Angie could come and listen. Their childhood was a constant reference between them, as if only those early memories, now so rehearsed, made the vexed era of adulthood more bearable.

The pub, two-storey with a beer garden, was one of Bev's haunts. Old-style unrenovated, working-class, Western Suburbs. She liked the rougher places, she said, where she saw the crims and the lowlifes she was trying to prosecute. 'Unnerves them, pisses them off, to have me turn up at their drinking holes.'

Ebbing light fell into the main bar through a glass sign that read *Coopers*, so that the room itself was coloured amber and frothy as light beer. There were three large TV screens showing an assortment of sports, and at the back a row of pokies, before which four hopeless men and one hopeful woman zealously sat. Through glass-panelled doors, what had once been the Ladies' Lounge, a sour, dim room of lilac and grey wallpaper, now stored kegs, crates and stacks of white plastic chairs. An old fellow was sitting asleep in the corner, slumped with his chin resting heavily on his chest. A brown glow rolled over him from the dusty lunette.

'I've been assigned to oversee this case because of the huge public interest,' Bev said. 'Just a matter of time. We sift all the stories and chuck out the nutters and eventually, with what's left, there'll be a few DNA checks to find the match. And we'll follow up certain related or non-related men. Blokes who claim to be an ex or a boyfriend are always worth a second look.' Bev turned around, checking, as if someone might be listening. 'The bigger mystery is what happened. Why she was out there and the type of crime. If she'd been a runaway, a captive, victim of a psycho, whatever.'

'Sam thinks this is daft, my wanting to know,' Angie offered. 'He said it'll be a long, boring search, with an anti-climax.'

'Yep. Sounds about right. Life's just like that.'

And they smiled at each other.

'So where is she now?'

'Still in the hospital, here in Sydney. It'll be a few weeks. She's dangerously underweight.'

'Any voice yet?'

'No, still no words. There's evidence that she's been subject to strangulation, and may have a permanently damaged voice box. Bruises, some old-looking, around the neck.' Bev took a swig of beer, then wiped her mouth as men do, with the back of her hand. 'Don't print that.'

'Of course.'

Bev realised she had said too much. 'Just don't.'

'It might not be published.' Angie sought to reassure. 'A feature piece, maybe not even that...' It sounded like a confession of incompetence. Not really a journalist anymore, now that she had gone freelance. Struggling to find what to say. Unsure of her focus. Secretly, she thought herself a failure, her portfolio of articles having been described by a senior editor as 'diverse'.

There were rumours that Jane had been discovered naked; some junior constable, seized with the frisson of mystery, had pretended to reveal insider knowledge to a paying journalist. So Bev was cautious. But she acknowledged Angie had somehow intuited the scene in the darkness, the almost-collision. 'How would you even guess?'

'Beats me.'

How to say that, in her imagining, Angie had glimpsed a fleshly truth? When she saw Jane in the wheelchair, she had no costume in which to clothe her: a woman from nowhere and unidentified, reduced to a figment under searing lights. Angie wanted to ask Bev for access to the list of those who had claimed to know Jane.

The pub was rowdy and airless. They were now competing with a rock-and-roll soundtrack and booming voices. Bev ordered a jug and suggested that they should move outside, to the beer garden. Happy Hour was almost over.

A young man at the bar called out. 'Trannie bingo later, Bev?'

'Fuck off, Jason.' Bev could handle herself. 'Arse-licker,' she added.

Angie was accustomed to her friend's language, with its spiky flounce. Godless profanity, her mum would have said.

The beer garden was quieter, and now Angie recalled standing at a pub doorway with her mother, scanning the crowd for her father, the acidic stink of it in her body and the clusters of burly men—glued in small, sweaty groups, leaning over drinks in hunchback formation, studiously ignoring them. But it was calmer here, the men younger and upright, and there were fake ferns nailed to the wall to indicate 'garden'. A few standing tables were set at a civil distance.

A sign read: *Wednesday! Schnitzel!*

It was easier to speak outside, to let their voices find lower tones in the descending night. Clearly, Bev was also captivated by Jane, by the sense of something monstrous behind the scant details, by the maw of possibilities, deep down and red. A woman about their age, in darkness, in the middle of nowhere. Angie saw the ditch again, and the heated car, and the strange man climbing down, as into a grave, to fling his dirty blanket.

The friends leaned their faces closer to confide. Angie watched Bev top up her glass. She hated beer. She felt conspicuous and out of place. Always, she thought, always out of place. Always this same, ungovernable feeling. And her past with Bev, centred on whispered compacts and breathy confessions, was receding now, dissolving, and seemed frail and fictitious.

'How's Sam?' Bev asked as they were parting.

Freelance meant poor, they said, in journalism talk. Don't do it. Madness. Angie was employed for a time with a respectable paper, then decided against all sensible advice to go freelance. She'd never much liked the word, with its mercenary associations, but wanted to follow the long form, not the compressed, story—the inconvenient, not the convenient. She believed in writing as revelation, and thought then—she still did—that our serious truths remain mostly hidden. How many other people really know us? How many? And was this not intolerable, to be largely unknown in the world? To have one's own account of the world barely uttered, or gone? All this she said to Sam, justifying her decision. She'd sounded high-minded, bloody-minded and sure. But she'd spent her time subbing, writing reviews and doing the occasional feature; to dignify what she did by calling it freelance was another kind of deception.

On grumpy days Sam claimed that she'd lost her way.

She'd lost credibility. 'So what are you lancing today?' he asked as he set off for school, where he struggled to teach sixteen-year-olds the glories of *Hamlet*. They would never pay off their mortgage at this rate. She would have to get a real job, he said, or at least something steady.

'Slings and arrows,' she called back, as he banged the door. Poor Hamlet, what a loser.

A sense of theatre was there from the start. So many who attached to Jane wanted the self-aggrandisement of putting their own loss at the centre of another's story. That the details were unknown made it democratic. Any dumb theory would work, any projection of need, any lust for solutions, any wish to placate a broken history or past mistakes. The quest for answers was itself old-fashioned and Angie felt uncomfortable entering the genre of 'true crime': styrofoam cups rolling in the wind; wannabe solvers of dodgy whodunnits, seekers of gory details, raincoated perves. Not really her thing. There was enough of it anyway, enough willed malfeasance out there to satisfy the grossest demand. And fiction: grimly Norwegian, darkly Finnish, wittily Scots. At some level she was appalled by the public appetite for stories of hurt, and by the addictive excellence of crime dramas on television.

Her marriage to Sam, which she'd always considered uncomplicated, was suffering complications. It seemed perverse to him that she would relinquish a safe job and head off with her lance, as he liked to say until it was no longer a joke. Angie had seen so many marriages founder, she was determined that hers would endure, so she went quiet, did not argue, and tried to pretend that she might change her mind. Children, she knew, would have made things easier, would have given them a reason to compromise for an imagined and expanding future. But after trying for ten years, they accepted that there would be no children, and each fell into their own lonely silence, admiring the pudgy, ugly babies of friends, then privately mocking when they came home. It was a relief, they agreed, not to have to deal with infant mess. Sam's disappointed parents, Nell and Mack, did not help at all. Nell would grab her arm and say dully, 'Still no news?'

After years of such comments, Angie grew distant and self-contained. Her own father was dead; her mother, Nora, also disappointed, lived a life of modest integrity in an outer suburb. She went to church each week, she shopped with a list, she helped her neighbour, almost ninety, with her straggly, dry garden, full of asters and dahlias that never quite reached full height. Nora had stopped asking. Philosophically, she accepted whatever Angie wanted; she told her daughter she was proud that she'd gone to university, proud too that they'd helped each other when her father had died, and that they'd wept together in complete understanding. Still, it would have been nice, a little kiddie playing with the hose, or squatting on the path to examine a lizard or a snail. Or reaching up to her, with a storybook, to say, 'Again, again!' as Angie once had.

'Proud of you, love,' Nora liked to repeat, so that Angie wouldn't get the wrong idea. She said her daughter was complete, no addition needed. She had made it clear she did not seek to possess her daughter's life.

Sam's younger brother, Mark, not the favourite, had three uncontrollable boys. Angie thought them hard to love. But she saw too how Sam looked on avidly as they grew, how he sat on the floor with them, found dopey topics of conversation, took pleasure in shopping for expensive, often sporty gifts. He was a wonderful uncle. These family matters, unresolved, troubled Angie in the middle of the night, stayed there, taunting, with what might have been a broader life, not this general sense of incompletion and thwarted love.

No telling. No telling of those shaming nights, when she remembered her body in a cramp, giving up blood and tissue. The ripple of her insides, turned to muck, and failing.

In their small terrace in Glebe, one bedroom, a living room and a courtyard with a square of tiles, they shared their lives. Moonlight in milky haze fell into their yard. Sitting together, outside, Angie listened to the traffic streaming densely in the parallel street, thought of the harbour and all those buildings they walked past to go down to the quay, the art deco cinema, now offices, the wool stores, now apartments, the warehouse and factory conversions in what had once been the working-class fringe of industrial life. The light rail snaked its slow path from the west to the water, and could be glimpsed shining with the fire of afternoon sun, pulling in a vibrating slide all the way to Central. Further on, the bigger shine of the sloshing harbour and passenger ferries in their watery trundle (spume unfurling behind, the bob-bob to another shore), and further still the glint of the heaving, ever-groaning Pacific.

Around them the streets sloped; some still held derelict terraces. But almost every week there was an old building newly boarded with planks and signs, waiting to be refashioned. Beyond that, the two bridges, and between them the skyscrapers, the casino and the glitter of impossible towers—another Sydney, tougher and more metallic, with which they had no connection. Angie saw it all like this, time-lapsed, day and night, and seen as if filmed from a swooping drone.

'So how did it go?' she asked.

'Most had heard the phrase "to be, or not to be" but hadn't a bloody clue what it meant, or why, or even where it came from. We make monologues all the time in our own heads, I told them. We tell ourselves our own lives, and sometimes our fears. We all have a secret voice. That seemed to stick.'

Angie knew that Sam was a good teacher; everyone said so. She liked this idea of confirming to kids that a story in the head was okay, that this was their own echo chamber of making or not making sense. 'Talking Heads, huh?'

Sam ignored the reference. 'And you?'

'Bev sends her love. She's a bit far from the action, here in Sydney, when the real investigation is in Broken Hill. Her job is to sift the Crime Stoppers calls and manage the case from central office. Some calls are a bit mad, and most want fiercely to claim Jane.'

'You too, maybe.' Diplomatically, Sam looked away. They had now entered the calm of their after-dinner peace talks.

'Yes. Me too.' She had a term in mind for her title, 'claimant', and knew that she was among their number.

When they'd first arrived here she told Sam of her city visions. She exaggerated, he said. She had a fear of change (incorrect); she was allergic (his word) to shiny towers (correct); her wish for sites and panoramas was a conservative fantasy (incorrect too, though on this she was less sure). Anticipating disapproval, she had never told him of her visits to the old Chinese temple, which, like her night walks, was a quirky, personal assertion. The temple stood gloriously in what she imagined as the centre of her suburb. It was like being elsewhere. Joss sticks, oriental lilies and piles of oranges at the altar, the spiralled incense, the pasted prayers, the side chapel dedicated to Departed Friends. It was vast, really, all that their talks hid or omitted.

And then later, in bed, she told him about *Wednesday! Schnitzel!* Making it into a casual amusement. He liked nonsense conjunctions. It was this texture of minor impressions that kept them in touch, that was, in a way, their essential connection. What she knew of her husband was mostly this: the small entertainments, the settled opinions, the grasp of shared principles. These days they rarely discussed matters of import, and Sam never sat down with her when she watched the news on television. He'd never consoled when something upset her, thinking it meaningless to care, except in theory, about what was so far away.

'The ghost, too,' he added, returning to his own story of the day. 'Of course I started with the ghost of the father, and that got them going. Ghosts, murder and madness: what's not to like?' He was smiling to himself. Angie thought of boys spinning their bikes on dirt and yelling to each other. She was vaguely aware of her own condescension. Aware too that there was respect here, in this marriage, but also heartache and suppression.

Sam shifted position in bed so that he faced away. Soon, listening to the steady rhythm of his breathing, his slide inside, Angie knew he'd fallen asleep and that she was alone again, wide awake. She felt aroused and abandoned. She understood how fundamentally hers was a physical attraction, that Sam had exerted a careless confidence with his body from the moment they first met, and this had made her feel desirable and trusting. She'd faltered in control by the force of her own desire. Made herself needy and greedy. Wanted more of the coming alive that he easily gave her. And now it was a kind of indifference he most often expressed, take it or leave it, distance, a preoccupation with matters not of passion, or their union, but of mundanity, she once accused him, in all its dull and stupid forms. Once said, she could not unsay it, and was mortified afterwards by her accusation. *Mundanity.* It meant nothing. It was her own wish for another life expressing itself as rude complaint. Marriages of a decade were destroyed for less; this gloom of worn expectations, this failure wholly to connect.

There were, of course, logistical issues to deal with. How to get the contact details of the claimants who were no longer 'persons of interest'. How to protect Bev as a source, if she gave up useful information. How to decide which of the punters would make good copy and deliver the requisite pathos, excitement and crazed speculation. Angie doubted the possibility of resolution, so knew that the tale of those around Jane, their desperation, would work better as a kind of reliable theme. Already she felt sure that Jane would never recover her power of speech, so that her story, in any case, would never be known.

It was something she would have liked to discuss with Sam: this silence. How silence figured in her past. How she remembered the prohibitions against speaking when her father was knocked out on the sofa, and her mother, in the muddle and flap of her wish to revive him, had put her finger to her lips to indicate *say nothing, not now, not later.* Nora was heedful of the community in which they were considered outsiders, what advice might be offered to her at the Country Women's

Association, what saving lie must be sustained (a medical condition picked up in Vietnam), what agitation there was in the simple act of wiping her husband's face with a flannel. For as long as she could remember, Angie had accepted her own smallness in this scene, and that she had been assigned a quiet destiny, her silence all that could be offered to this wretched version of family life.

It was another month before Bev released a few names or addresses. These poor souls, wanting a connection, had been conclusively ruled out; no harm could come from allowing Angie to meet them. But knowing the risk she was taking, Bev covered herself. She prepared a statement for each to sign saying they understood that their role in the investigation was over; they consented to share their information and meet a journalist interested in the case. There was no obligation to follow up if they felt the issue was closed. Nothing to lose, Bev said, for either of us, as long as they sign.

It was hardly by the book, but Bev would be in the clear. All she had done, after all, was give out Angie's phone number to anyone who felt the need to speak further or explain why they had come forward. Their decision, not hers. Like passing on the name of a counsellor.

The first caller was a man named Herb. Angie agreed to meet him at Circular Quay. He liked a cafe down there, he said on the phone, and wanted her to know his side of the story. He sounded assured and credible. It was a day of seething rain and winds whipping through the concourse and the ferry terminals. Sheets of water flew up the sea wall and across the concrete walkway. Perky wavelets sprung everywhere; the ferries tossed side to side. Already Angie felt caught in a fool's errand. Her shoes were soaked. Her umbrella was inside out. The gods were against them. Even though the meeting place was a street back from the water, the churn of the harbour was audible, and a sense of unrest was all about.

The cafe was full of disheartened tourists, sheltering against the weather. They'd come to take snaps of the Opera House and had been blown dripping indoors. Coffee, not ice cream. No sunshine here.

Herb was perhaps mid-sixties and had a Brummy accent. Rheumy eyes behind owlish glasses, an unfashionable, scraggy moustache. He claimed to have migrated to Australia as a child, but Angie thought that unlikely, given the obduracy of his vowels and his English manner. He had worn a tie. No Australian man wore a tie to a cafe. She suspected Herb was a fantasist, and perhaps wasting her time.

He shook his umbrella and sprayed water all over the table, then wiped and dabbed with his sleeve like a sit-com waiter. A waitress arrived to take his umbrella, stowing it in a bucket near the door. Something told Angie he was a regular, tolerated for his eccentricities.

She placed her phone on the table and Herb consented to

be recorded.

He was the first of many who would tell Angie he was in love with Jane, except in this case she was Liz, and he had met her back in the old country—when he visited, he added swiftly, for a short holiday. Liz worked as a shop assistant in the pharmacy where he picked up his meds. She'd been shy at first, but gradually they got talking and discovered they had shared interests: kittens, gambling and space exploration.

Herb's tone was upbeat, almost jolly, telling the story of a romance. 'Here,' he said, 'a photo to show that she's Liz. My girlfriend.'

Herb presented a photograph taken in someone's grimy backyard in the Black Country. It was one of those images both bleached and tinged yellow with age. A low sky, a sooty prospect of what might have been Wolverhampton, with brick chimneys and a factory visible above the fence line in the distance. Herb was definitely Herb; Liz was nothing like Jane. Each was dressed in the clothes of youth.

'We wanted a babby,' Herb said sadly. 'Then she disappeared.'

He was stirring his tea with slow deliberation. The concentration of his effort seemed to Angie disproportionate.

'And when was this?'

'Thirty years ago now. She's been missing for thirty years. I've nothing to prove that poor lady on the telly is Liz. But I know she is, I know it deep in my bones. And the awful thing is that they won't let me see or talk to her, so she will never know I'm here. She will never know I'm still waiting.'

Herb gave a sort of grunt, then a snuffle, then began softly to cry. In a show of resignation, he lowered his forehead to the table, wombat-like, to hide his distress. Angie found it hard to comprehend the magnitude of his delusion: clearly he'd not appreciated the passage of time, that Liz would be his age now, not Jane's. Such an obvious discrepancy seemed almost comically woeful.

Eventually, still insistent, he raised his head. 'So, can you help?'

No, she could not. She could not help. Angie looked away so as not to meet his hurt, red eyes.

It had been a dreadful meeting. This man was by turns piteous, deranged and pleading. Could she even include Herb in any story, so exiled from reason and common sense? It would be unkind to point out to him that his quest was a denial of time, and that what had been shattered thirty years ago could not be restored.

No, she could not help him, but was sorry for his loss, she responded, as if speaking of one recently dead.

Herb appeared unbalanced as he stood when they parted ways, then found his body again, straightened his intention and set off in a kind of march. The rain was lighter, reduced to a drizzle, and he had forgotten or neglected to unfurl his umbrella, which swung metronomic against his thigh. Former military, perhaps? The tie and trousers too, Angie thought again: completely inappropriate. Herb was heading towards

George Street at a quickening pace, and gradually he was screened by the rain's silver light.

The second caller was a woman called Vesna. She was somewhere in rural Victoria and was not able to meet in person, but wished, with dauntless urgency, to speak on the phone. She agreed to be recorded.

'*Vesna* means "spring" in Croatian,' she volunteered. She was staking a claim. She was affirming for some reason the importance of her origin.

'And what,' Angie asked carefully, 'is your connection to Jane?'

'Twin,' was the surprise answer. 'Her name is Marta. Non-identical, of course. If you see me you will say no, that is not Marta's sister, but we were born five minutes apart in Zagreb, thirty-five years ago, and eleven years before my parents migrated. I have the birth certificates. I can show you. Have you been to Zagreb?' Vesna didn't wait for an answer. 'The most beautiful city in Europe. The cathedral. The old town. The shrine to the virgin. The Sava. Have you been? You should go. Everyone should go. The Museum of Broken Relationships, unique to Zagreb. We care, you see. We want to preserve bits and pieces, and when Marta went missing in Melbourne there was nothing to say where, and we could not tolerate this, me and my parents, so we put advertisements in all the papers, both English and Croatian. But not a thing, not one response, *ništa*, nothing. The police, they did nothing, I tell you.'

Vesna drew breath and continued: 'Fuck the Australian police, who do nothing at all, and last month I come all the way to Sydney to see Marta, and I go to the station this time, and I shout at them and they say, "Lady, calm down now," like I know nothing, am nothing, like our suffering is nothing to them. With this Jane, I say it is Marta, I say I know, I know her—who knows better than the one who shared a womb, and who grew up together and who dreams every night that she returns from being lost? When she can speak again, she will speak Croatian, and she will say, "I am Marta, sister of Vesna," and they will know then they have been wrong.'

'How long ago,' Angie asked, 'did Marta go missing?'

'We were twenty, we were living in Broadmeadows then. She got in with bad people, crooks and druggies, the lot of them. I told the police fifteen years ago. But what did they do? They did nothing. Nothing.'

'Did you give a DNA sample?'

'I did the swab thing when Marta was first registered as missing person and they said it was still on records. Offered to show me. But then they say no match. I say impossible, impossible, we are twins, I know her anywhere, my sister; impossible! I think they destroyed my sample to cover corruption in the drug squad. I think they knew something back then, fifteen years ago, and they are still covering up, they are all guilty as hell.'

There was a fury in Vesna's voice that prevented questions.

'They won't let me see her or talk to her, so she will never know I'm looking. I think maybe they have drugged her so she will not recognise me. I think maybe they are covering their arses and will probably have me killed now, for all what I know.'

And now Vesna at last went silent. Angie heard what sounded like rustling paper. And a flutter, which may have been tissues, or pages, or shreds of thin, papery hope falling into an abyss. She was filled with a sense of having nothing to offer.

Again came the same question: 'Do you think you can help me?'

And Angie said no, she was just a journalist. Not even employed. Freelance.

'Write my side,' said Vesna, 'so if something happens to me, or to Marta, we have a record. Bad people, the police. You cannot trust them.'

Vesna texted Angie her address and phone number. Then the names and addresses of her parents, now returned to Zagreb. She had added a thumbs-up emoji, a pink love heart and an exclamation mark.

When she closed her phone Angie wondered what this woman looked like, if she was anything like Jane, if there had been something in the advertised face that had gripped Vesna in the way infirmity in a child inspires attachment and the wish to donate to a good cause. Or, more troubling, she may have seen a true resemblance. Perhaps this woman, still raging, still wanting her sister, saw the marvellous return. *Believed* that she saw the marvellous return.

The third on the list, Marie, rang to say she knew that Jane was not her Sal, but she wanted to talk anyway. It was important to keep the issue of missing persons in the press. Could they meet?

It was another cafe, not far from Redfern Station. Angie walked there, timing well, but had a last-minute panic when she couldn't locate the cafe. She opened her phone to discover that she was standing close by—in the satellite's clever eye she was the vivid blue spot, arrived. Later, she would tell Sam it was the most nondescript cafe in Sydney, a place poor-looking, with old, faded signage and tucked veils of shadow. It might have been the front for some other business or purpose.

Inside hung fusty air and walls painted a dark reddish colour. There was a metal ice cream sign that would nowadays be a coveted collectible, and a pressed-tin ceiling of acanthus leaf design. Vintage, possibly nineteen-twenties, when acanthus still referenced the columns and classicism of a swanky joint. And Angie felt it: the comfort of dehistoricised spaces, the low light transmitting an enveloping calm.

At the back stood a counter, and behind it the Vietnamese proprietor. She was surprised when Angie entered and gave a slight nod. An old lady with a friendly, open face. Her thin, grey hair was combed into a chignon that resembled a golf ball.

Marie was seated with a cup of tea. There were no other customers. When Angie entered, Marie didn't rise in acknowledgement but indicated the seat opposite. 'Mrs Nguyen is my friend,' she said. And, hearing her name, Mrs Nguyen became alert.

Angie ordered Vietnamese coffee. 'I love the condensed milk.' It was a stupid thing to say. Infantile.

Marie took no notice. She was a middle-aged woman, downcast and bent, and the subdued angle of her body, a disconsolate slouch, reminded Angie of someone she could not now recall. Marie seemed in no hurry to begin their conversation. They waited until Mrs Nguyen brought the glass with the condensed milk and pushed the metal coffee filter on top. Slowly, she poured hot water into the filter.

'*Cà phê sua dá*,' she said softly, obliging Angie to listen.

The light in the cafe was pewter, leaning in sideways from the busy street. They sat in silence until the coffee had ceased its drip-drip-drip.

'So it's like this,' said Marie. 'Jane would be about the same age as my daughter, Sal, who went missing years ago, as a fourteen-year-old. Police said "runaway" and that she'd eventually return, but she never returned and went into the Missing Persons' file. A policeman here at Redfern, a lovely bloke, Detective Fitzgerald, took a special interest in the youngsters who disappeared for no reason. We're still in touch and sometimes he has tea with me here, at Mrs Nguyen's. It was Bob Fitzgerald who told me about Jane on the telly. Bob is retired now but took me down to the station and made sure they checked my DNA was still on their database, but they said—definitively—that Jane was not my daughter. I had studied her face in the paper and knew that already. I thought, *No, that's not her*, but I had to be sure, you see—and Bob, of course, Bob had to be sure too. I did it for Bob. I think maybe he took others with missing girls or sisters down to the station. It's his mission, you know, to find these lost people. I'm not the only person who has someone missing.'

Angie was unsure what to ask. She didn't want to intrude into a grief so guarded and austere. In the distance sounded the dull surf of the trains arriving and leaving.

At last Angie asked, 'Do you mind passing on Bob's details?'

'Not a problem. Bob is still working behind the scenes. He thinks there's not enough attention given to Missing Persons. Obvious crime is a bigger story. A shooting in the Western Suburbs, a fancy store robbed. The missing are less newsworthy. They're often kids, you know, or mob, or people no one really cares about. The homeless. Druggies. Bob has kept me going. We all love Bob.'

There was pause. And then, sensing how her misfortune kept her closed, Angie knew what to ask. 'Tell me a little about Sal. Only if you want to.'

Now they connected. Now there was a kind of relief, and an exhalation. For the first time since they had met, Marie looked at Angie directly.

'Sal was such a pretty little girl. It made her a target, you know? To be pretty like that. Even as a toddler her curls attracted attention, and she was trusting and smiled easily at any old stranger. I tried to warn her, of course, but what can you do? A child like that. Smiley and pretty and full of beans. She wasn't a runaway, she was taken, that much I'm sure of, and it was too horrible to imagine, so I just emptied out, over the years. Maybe somewhere she has a new life, with a little one of her own, and maybe she'd had enough of the city and went bush, or maybe fruit picking up north, or off with mates on a jaunt in the back of a ute.'

Here there was a longer pause, since Marie clearly did not believe her own happier story and was reluctant to speak of her darkness, or to describe her fears.

'She knows where I am,' added Marie. 'I've never moved, just in case. Just in case she's still alive and comes searching one day.'

Marie finished her tea. Her hands were now unsteady and she hid them beneath the table. The reserve cultivated by patience was near collapse. Then she readjusted. 'What interested me about Jane was that she appeared. Mostly it's stories of disappearance. Now an appearance.' It might have been a vision she saw, given such meaningful pause. 'There's some lucky mum out there. Some family, soon back together.'

Angie then said a little about herself, and how she knew the detective on television, her friend from childhood. Another of the good ones, like Bob. She tried to make herself plausible, and not to overstate, or intrude, or make any promises.

Marie stood when Angie gathered her bag and sunglasses to leave. Angie did not wish to prolong what she understood was a kind of courtesy, this woman speaking so plainly and without drama, saying to another, a stranger, how hard it was, her loss, and how bleakly persisting.

Angie placed her fingertips very lightly on the older woman's arm. 'Thank you.' In some obscure way she felt indebted. Marie had made no special plea or appeal but was enclosed in her own stoicism.

Marie lifted her cup and Angie's glass to take them to Mrs Nguyen, assisting her friend as if they were alone in a domestic kitchen. Busy, cleaning up, fussing at the counter, she seemed momentarily to have recovered her self-possession. Her hands came to rest when she became aware that her dissembling against grief was done for the time being.

Angie set off to walk home, crossing onto Lawson Street, past the slogans and murals that stretched in red, yellow and black across the railway bridge. *Say kNOw to drugs. 40,000 years is a long time.* Below, the tracks fanned and meshed their iron arms back towards Central, or on routes to Strathfield, Parramatta,

Emu Plains, Penrith. These names were spots on a line indicating order and progression, not the disarray of rush hour or drunken misbehaviour, or crowds in team scarves and raucous accord, crushed together in a pack to get to the weekend rugby league. A deception here: this peace of surfaces, this calm of distance. Angie watched passengers moving on the stairs to and from the platforms, all carrying their human disorder inside them.

And now, with her own disorder, she headed through the shady, doglegged backstreets under the peeling paperbarks, which smelled of must and dirt, and now and then of vagrant piss. The paths were cracked by tree roots and strewn with fallen leaves. At some random moment a racket of cicadas sounded, discharging in unison their fricative dialect. The chorus was swollen and grating; it throbbed with an alien rasp. And when at last it ceased, in a tremulous interval, the image she had seen on television a few weeks ago recurred: the man who sat very still, bent over, and who knew that his family was dead. Something in the angle of the shoulders, carrying a load, had connected him to Marie.

That evening, Angie spoke to Sam about Marie. Sam listened patiently and did not interrupt, but when she finished her account of their meeting he asked why she would interview a woman who sounded so ordinary, of so little of interest, and with no actual news or information to impart. His tone was sulky, his mood unsympathetic. 'Wasting your time.' This compulsion to spoil what had moved her.

'Not at all,' she said weakly.

And he stood above her, frowning.

It was hard to know what to say in response. To Angie, Marie had seemed an exemplar; she waited in dignity with the barest skerrick of hope; she arranged her life with small ceremonies, like tea in the company of Mrs Nguyen; she honoured her detective friend, who was devoted to the missing. Marie had known beyond doubt that Jane was not her Sal, but had still blessed, in her own mind, the true mother who might greet her. She had bestowed what she longed for. This was not ordinary. This was saving grace.

Asperity, thy name is Sam.

After he went to bed, Angie stayed up, laptop open, following residual ideas. The night was noisy with squalls and the thrash of street trees. Camphor laurels. Figs. The jacaranda on the corner. Bats flitted eastwards, veering off course in the wind, and possums now and then distantly coughed.

The small triangular park up the road hosted a community of possums: she only saw them occasionally, very late at night. Once, when she opened the front door, a grey brushtail was squatted on the pavement before her. Immobile, dumb-looking and unfazed, it stared at her for what felt like a full minute. Then the possum ambled off, lackadaisical, its attitude sneaky, its tail wagging in a lazy, almost insolent swing. It was as curious as she to see another species in the dark. Such beady eyes, ashine, and with such a fixed gaze.

Superstitious, Angie rose and opened the front door. There was no possum. No symbolic or friendly animal visitor. There was nothing but the windy hollow of the city's loud darkness. The front step was like a cliff she might one day walk over.

The city was so alive to her at night. Everything claimed a greater propinquity. Everything achieved the shivering quality of things coming into being. Sometimes she felt like a poet, not a journalist. She saw the rhymes and connections between unlike things. She felt the moon slide, and the kick and slobber of a dreaming dog, and the passionfruit vine against the back fence uncurling its looped tendrils. Jasmine flowers, palely visible, and white moths gliding in circles. Bat-squeak in the sky, infant cries somewhere, and far off, the weather-change rolling in from the Pacific.

She sensed things in resonance. She sensed the turn of lovers in their beds, made hot with each other's bodies. She sensed grander things too, unity, peace. Night made her romantic. Sometimes, very late, she felt the presence of something whispered, something airy, which she thought of as safekeeping. This was her yearning for a capitalised world: Unity, Peace, Safekeeping.

Since the Jane event, unrest had blown in the wind. Angie resisted analysing what was possibly a crass projection. Preoccupation was a necessary skill for her work, but there was a faltering here too, a condition of things losing solidity.

The walls of their house might have been made of cardboard and string.

She turned from the front door and moved back to the kitchen table. *Back to the facts*, she told herself. She located the website of the Museum of Broken Relationships. It was a real place, in Zagreb, where miserable people deposited small objects saved from the ruins of love. Objects of sentimental importance, or everyday things that took on an aura of extraordinary emotional power. His toothbrush. Her hairclip. The pile of socks, still there in the laundry when the couple had split. The single glove, lambswool and soft, discovered under the sofa. The empty cigarette box he had flung away during their last argument. The tacky red keepsake, a useless wooden plaque, from their first holiday together, in southern Spain. One of the exhibits was a tiny bottle of tears; another an axe, which a German woman had used to destroy her husband's bespoke furniture, then left the splintered remains for his mistress to collect. Some objects were tinted with dejection or teary regret, some with aggression, violence and a wish to harm. Angie thought it a depressing site, made for the madly inconsolable. Why would anyone want to visit this broken-hearted collection?

Lacrimarium: a glass vial in which, in ancient Rome, tears were preserved. Still used, apparently. This was a furtive, private act that Angie could imagine trying—catching the physical evidence of inadmissible feeling. Her temperament led others to think her perpetually composed; sometimes she would have liked to contradict them.

The Museum of Broken Relationships was the kind of factoid she and Sam might have shared in the past. They would have made jokes and come up with their own clever list. They would have outdone each other inventing preposterous items that indicated that objects have memory too. That objects contain sentiment. That objects, even trivial ones, made of moulded cheap plastic, like a toy or a toothbrush, or a ball of hair, or a torn photograph, persist in the realm of loss as if evolving organisms. There might have been a proclamation on the museum wall: *See how feeble human feelings are alongside the tenacity of objects*.

She would not tell Sam now about the Museum of Broken Relationships. Credulous and afraid, vigilant of his feelings, she felt keenly the need to protect them both.

Angie rose and opened the front door again. There was still nothing there but the wind, and the vacant street, and the enormous night. She was impatient with her own inability to stay still. Then, as if summoned, there appeared a grinning black dog, trotting alone on the street, with no owner in sight. Light shone in an undulating saddle on its back. It turned its head slightly and gave her a scornful glance.

The fourth interview was with Jake, another man searching for his girlfriend. Jake rang and asked to meet at his local, a pub at Liverpool, in the west of the city, a train ride away. Angie agreed; she wanted to show Sam that she was serious, and that there was an intelligent motive behind recording interviews with those who were disappointed and bereft. It was all she had to go on, really.

Situated on the highway, so that there was the sound of traffic, like distant thunder, noticeable even inside, the pub was pure seventies brutalism: blond brick, a frugal rectangle, strict utility. Rugby league posters decorated the dingy foyer, the Liverpool All Saints in collective ziggurats and singular mugshots, along with banners, plaques and gaudy advertisements. No trannie bingo here, but a meat raffle on Thursdays (*Thursday! Meat raffle!* What was it with exclamation marks?) and volunteers wanted for the Junior League.

Angie gazed around the bar and again found herself the odd one out. There were two other women, not counting the tired-looking barmaid. It was quiet—ten-thirty am—and there were only seven in the bar. But the barmaid had clearly been told to look out for her.

'You here for Jake? Go through.' She indicated a side door, which opened onto what seemed like a committee room: ten chairs, a long oval table, a jug of water in the centre. A clean, well-lit place.

Jake was scrolling on his phone and leapt to attention. He held out his hand as he introduced himself. 'Bin Ahmed, Jake bin Ahmed.' Angie was curious about his ethnicity, but it would have been rude to ask. She noticed his receding hairline and wispy hair; he was olive-skinned, a handsome man, on the wrong side of forty. She had assumed he was unemployed, being able to meet in the morning, but now reconsidered: he was well-dressed, confident and self-assured, and without the manner or appearance of those impoverished or out of work.

Jake asked if she wanted a coffee, and when she said yes he ducked out to place the order. They made small talk about the trains until the barmaid came with a tray and two cups.

'Thanks, Lee.'

He apologised for the meeting place. He was not a drinker himself, he said, but knew the owners of the pub, and from time to time it was convenient to use this room, which was quiet and close to where he worked.

Angie knew there was a protocol to observe, as with Marie, and took her time. Calmly, she said to Jake, 'So how do you know Jane?'

'Jane is Fatimah,' he said. 'Eurasian, like me. We're both originally from Malaysia and we first met in KL. I am trying still to establish her identity, and for a while I was what police call a "person of interest". If I was really her boyfriend, they said, I was automatically a "person of interest".'

Jake's candour surprised Angie; this was the kind of detail most men would choose to hide.

'Her family are back in KL and they disagreed; they said, "This woman is not our Fatimah and this man is a liar and unworthy." After she appeared, Fatimah's father flew all the way to Sydney to check. I know he visited the police station and spoke to the officers there. I probably remain a "person of interest" because I love her. Because I have shown my concern so openly.'

'Jake?'

'Jake is my English name, of course. Fatimah's English name is Lynette. Jake and Lynette.' He sipped his coffee thoughtfully. 'And this issue of names and places seems to confuse everyone. It is hard to explain to those born here, or those whose migrancy is less complex.'

'So when did Lynette—Fatimah—go missing?'

'Almost seven years ago. Australia disappointed us, so we moved to Penang for a while, where I had business contacts. Import/export. But she wanted to return to Sydney and base the business here, so I agreed. We found this community in the Western Suburbs and decided to settle. That was ten years ago. We were fine, we were settled; then she disappeared.'

'Did you tell the police?'

'Of course. She's an official Missing Person. Not unknown but missing. I know her. I know Fatimah. I was investigated when I first reported her missing. A brown man, you know? Unworthy. *Untrustworthy*.'

Angie waited, unsure what to say next. She expected Jake to produce a photograph to prove his claim.

'Can you help?' he asked. Straight to the expected question.

'I'm interviewing others who claim a connection with Jane. I'm not judging and not advocating; I'm simply a journalist.'

Jake looked disappointed. 'But my story is the true one,' he said. 'I think no one in the police force wants to imagine their captive Jane might be a migrant.'

Captive Jane. The phrase struck like a blow and troubled her. And he was right; there was a captive quality to this woman she'd not yet considered.

Jake handed her a business card and rose, checking his watch. It had been like a business meeting to him, after all; direct, straight-talking, what can you do for me? Angie was impressed but a little unnerved by his brusque and busy manner. He thanked Lee as he left—a courteous man—and she was pleased to be acknowledged, holding up the glass she was cleaning to offer a sparkly wave.

The card read *Abdul bin Ahmed: Importer/Exporter*. Addresses in Kuala Lumpur and in Sydney. Abdul. Abdul and Fatimah.

On the train, returning, Angie wondered how much she might have missed. The television glimpse of Jane hadn't yielded specific racial clues or the nuances of an obvious identity. Bev had not mentioned the issue of race. Made sallow and flat by the lights, nullified by silence, or by others describing her, she had retained the tag of simplification. Perhaps, Angie realised now, she had also been somehow deracialised. In British crime shows, 'IC7 female' was a woman of unknown ethnicity. She remembered those codes, those categorical descriptors. And then felt ashamed of herself. This was the reductive model her writing had taught her to avoid. Don't make a person a category.

The man who almost ran down Jane in the middle of the night and then 'saved her'—his words—was Terry Williams, Tezza to his mates. Officially, he was not free to speak, being still designated a 'person of interest'. Angie wondered how he knew her phone number and her role, and what had impelled him to make contact. Perhaps he wished to manage his story for some future account of the event.

They met at a seat in the Botanical Gardens that faced the harbour—his choice.

'Tezza,' he said, extending his hand. 'Visiting Sydney to see me cousin.'

Nervous at first, he rambled a little on the yachts and the ferries, brightly visible, pushing away into the blue distance. He was afraid of water, he confessed, since he had never learned to swim. 'But look at them go!'

Tezza seemed to have been designed to match a stereotype. He was a carrot-top Aussie in shorts and T-shirt, no-nonsense, jokey, with half an ear sliced away and blazing scars on his nose from the removal of incipient skin cancers. A bushman. A bloke. He sat beside her wasted, reeking and shy. About fifty, perhaps more. Hard to say with bushmen.

Angie was suspicious of him from her first imaginings—she would concede this now. But with him, listening, she saw that he was a hapless fellow, still disturbed by all that was inexplicable in what he had seen, unable to stop talking about it, still shaken to the core by an apparition that had in fact scared him. He was a man—she saw it now, clear as day—bewildered and confused by his own incredulity.

'She was that skinny,' he said. 'It was like seeing a skeleton. I thought, *Fuck me, what the fuck is this?* And I slammed on the brakes and only just stopped in time, and she showed no fear, nothing at all really, but only wobbled a bit, then fell over. I tell you now, I was pretty freaked out. What the fuck?

'I thought maybe she had died in the ditch and I didn't want to touch her. I guess I was shit-scared. The voice on the phone said, "Check her breathing," but I couldn't see any breathing and I thought, *Bloody hell, she's not breathing at all, and maybe the coppers will think it was me, that I did something wrong.* I didn't really look at her then, only later, when I was waiting for the ambulance to arrive, and I sat there in the ditch with her and with my phone light I looked at her face, I took a peek and saw she was youngish, eyes closed, dead still. She was real to me then, and I started to cry.

'Please don't write this down, but I blubbed like a baby. I turned off the light and there I was in the darkness, sitting on the dirt next to the poor lady under my stinky blanket, and I was blubbing away. The night seemed so big and we both seemed so small, and I was pretty sure she would die, if she wasn't already dead, and that maybe I would be blamed and I would have to answer questions—I did anyway, fucking police—and I felt guilty, somehow, even though I done nothing wrong, and I swear to you, all I did was sit there not touching anything until the ambulance came. It was like time stopped still and I was stuck there, thinking about death. I was pretty freaked out, I can tell you.'

Tezza was wringing his hands and staring down at his boots, returned not to Jane but to his own scene of distress.

'And by the time the ambo touched my elbow I was shaking and a bit out of it, and he wrapped me in one of those golden blankets, like I was the one rescued, like I was the sick one. There were two ambos, and together they put the lady on a stretcher and pulled her up to the road, and then, bloody hell, they said I shouldn't drive, shock or something, exposure maybe, or some other thing—anyway, they wouldn't let me, so I had to sit in the back of the ambulance in this awful bright light with the lady I didn't want to look at. She had one of those oxygen mask things over her face, and she was totally out of it, but I knew then that she wasn't dead, or they wouldn't have used the mask...And I had to leave my car on the side of the road, in the dark, I had to leave my car...'

They were both silent for a minute. Tezza had finished his testimony and would say no more. He was now examining his hands, turning them, searching for something not there.

'Red Ford Falcon?' Angie asked.

'Yeah,' he said, impressed. 'How did you know?'

'It was behind you in the clip I saw on television. Your car.'

'Ah, yeah.' Pleased she'd noticed, and understood his pride. 'Like a detective, huh?'

Now he lifted his face and gazed again across the water. Ferries and yachts and light bursting, close in and far away.

Before Sam came home in the afternoon, Angie put on her music. Talking Heads. The first track she went to was 'And She Was'. Angie bopped in the front room, forgetting herself as seen, dancing like no one was watching because no one was watching. And she was, and she was, and she was—the refrain. In the video clip, there was a cartoon in which a woman, unseen but for her feet, floated around her city, entering and leaving spaces, rising between houses, over parks and gardens, then at last flying up like a spirit into outer space. The combination of change and repetition had been transfixing. And she was, and she was, and she was.

Angie and Bev had danced to the song in Grade Seven. It was still on the radio in 1990 and they performed in Bev's bedroom, mouthing the words, becoming a she who was everywhere and endlessly transformable. Both girls loved to dance. They flung themselves about and mimicked the figures on television. They heedlessly embraced, they venerated the lead singer, they enjoyed the sway of their own hips and their fitful prancing.

Bev's mum would yell, 'Turn it down!' and they did for a while, but gradually, by stealth, re-pumped up the volume.

And so Angie danced. She stepped lightly around the sofa

and the chairs, she pointed at the television, she pouted, she held out her arms, flung wide and was released, if just a little, into a younger self. As she spun, she entered a kind of sincerity. This disinhibition, this voluptuary of movement: this had once been a truth for her.

Sam unlocked the front door. He heard the music, saw her sweaty and puffed with her own amusement. He dropped his bag near the door and threw his keys onto the sideboard. 'Good to see that you're working hard too.' Tetchy. Tired.

Sam's irritation was now a practised response. It entered the house with him and Angie felt his derision like a blast. She switched off the music. Sam said something she didn't hear. He had already turned away. And this turning away—this was what their marriage had become.

It was a scorching day, but hazy and steaming after an early downpour. Bob Fitzgerald, the Redfern policeman, now retired, shuffled to a seat in the park. He chose the driest bench and spread his newspaper, for good measure, then gestured to Angie to join him. It was his way, she decided; he was instinctively kind.

Lugubrious and withdrawn, grey and grizzled, he looked uncomfortable in what might have been brand-new trousers; he kept plucking at the seams and realigning the waistband. He also had a habit, when thinking, of patting his wristwatch.

Angie liked him immediately: unassuming, keen to help, modest about his own role.

'Marie seemed to like you,' he began.

Angie took this as meaning that she might be trusted, that Marie knew she hadn't wanted to exploit, to sensationalise or to cheat.

'I'm just a freelancer,' she said, aware of her apologetic tone. 'I was initially drawn to this idea of a woman turning up out of nowhere; now I see how many others took notice, and wanted to know if she was theirs.'

It sounded weak and redundant. Angie fiddled with her phone and tapped the recorder. She had never been good with authority figures, and even a kind retired policeman made her feel self-conscious.

Bob was turning his watchband. Then he patted his watch. 'Me too—I'm a kind of freelancer now.' He waited to see if Angie would respond. 'I've known Marie from the beginning,' he said, 'from before Sal went missing. She's a good sort, Marie, what they call a pillar of her community, always helping others. But no one thought much of kids going astray in those days. Sometimes they went up north, to pick fruit for a few weeks—it was a thing, back then—and returned with money burning a hole in their pocket. I suggested that to Marie, but we both knew that wasn't Sal. She humoured me, I guess.

'Then eventually Sal was an official Missing Person. Marie did her own investigation, knocking on doors, asking anyone who might have known her, making posters to fix on poles and in shop windows. She had more energy than the force, I can tell you. After a couple of years, she was too sad, and for a while she didn't speak to anyone much.

'Mrs Nguyen—you met her? They became pals and I think that helped. I don't know Mrs Nguyen's background, but something connects them. Eventually Marie went back to community work and volunteering.'

'I was wondering about you,' Angie said. 'About your role in all this.'

And now Bob glanced away. 'Not much, really.'

Both were silent. Bob patted his watch. The direct question had thrown him sideways. For a moment they just sat.

'I lost my own boy when he was ten.' Bob stared into the sky.

Jesus, thought Angie, *another one*.

'Not what you think.' Bob was quiet, still looking away, then regained his composure. A cop's instinct, Angie thought: don't make it personal. 'But I decided to move to outreach policing and ended up with Missing Persons. Most of my colleagues didn't want a bar of it—not enough results, tedious, they said, and dealing all the time with hysterical parents or rabid siblings. Not my words, you understand.

'I knew Sal,' he added. 'Or remember her, anyway. A real charmer, she was, and a bit of a firecracker with the other kids. Hard to miss, Sal. Marie and Sal adored each other. I can't imagine Sal just running off. Ever. I think Marie knew this, and that I believed her, which is why we teamed up.' A pause.

'But we didn't get a result, as we say in the force.'

And here, for a brief time, Bob choked up. Angie saw his embarrassment. She saw how he fought for self-control. She saw too that he felt his career was a failure, that something about this case in particular—something about Sal in particular—was a burden he still carried. After all these years he still carried a ghost child. Or two.

He ran both his hands over his grey head, as if pressing down his feelings. Like a sage, world-weary and overcome. Another wait. Then Bob said, 'I can't help you. A retired copper can't get access to any information. Just so you know.'

Ah, the question reversed. Had he imagined she was asking for help?

'It's a story,' Angie insisted. 'I'm only a journalist.'

'Yep, I know.' Bob found a handkerchief in his pocket and blew his nose. Again, he turned away. Another kind of turning. She could see it now: a man of intermittent but perpetual mourning. He was bracing himself against memory, against unforgetting. Against whatever flew at him unheralded and entered his head.

When Bev and Angie next met it was at Bev's apartment, for a pizza.

Girls' night, Bev called it; both needed to talk. They were alike in wanting the other to confirm what Angie called constitutional seriousness, how they had seen in each other—perhaps from the beginning, and certainly before they had words for it—the ability to not look away, to search for deeper meanings, to take themselves seriously. 'Un-Australian,' Bev liked to call it. Sometimes this idea was the cause of hilarity; sometimes Bev and Angie, at the end of a long talk, had a drink and toasted 'constitutional seriousness', both pleased to have a friend with whom to discuss what is seldom expressed, those dark, churning thoughts that turned in the night like sticky clay, like the cling of the earth itself, like the sightless underground world, loss, poor decisions, miscarriages, grief. The way nothing fitted together. The way beauty might be convulsive. The way sadness might be pious. The command of godforsaken things to be noticed and to matter.

It was possible, said Bev, that they courted each other's sorrow. Angie was impressed by this idea and by her friend's formulation, as if wanting to make their conversation another version of romance. Bev had understood Angie when she mentioned the snow man—how a few seconds on the telly, of a man huddling in a white blur, might stay for weeks as the trace of historical pain. They had known each other *forever*, Bev liked to say; and this too, this sense of an ineradicable and layered time that might exist between friends, this also seemed an essential truth operating in how they spoke to each other. In what it was possible to say.

Bev handed Angie a glass of shiraz before she sat down.

So this would be one of those indeterminate meetings, a little inebriated and a little serious. The pizza had already arrived and lay in its soggy box, oil staining the table, a great wheel of cholesterol and deeply inviting. No fake virtue of an accompanying salad. Just a box and a pizza.

'Busy day,' said Bev, by way of explanation.

They ate in silence at first, each preoccupied.

And then Angie asked, 'Any more news about Jane?'

Bev declared she wasn't prepared to 'talk shop' all night, but clearly she needed to say something of her own courted sorrow. 'Confidential?'

'Of course.'

'Those early bruises, yes: it was strangulation. And she's given birth at some stage, not too long ago. So maybe a child somewhere.'

'Jesus.'

It was clear Bev was conflicted but felt compelled to tell Angie these details. It was an unsolved case so she was breaching any number of professional protocols. Angie wondered if Bev had been drinking before she arrived: copper's medicine, she would call it, at the end of a hard day.

'She was severely malnourished, as you know, and there's X-ray evidence of past fractures. Hard to imagine exactly what Jane has suffered. The team in Broken Hill have come up with bugger-all.'

'No words?'

'Still silent. There's only so much you can tell from a live body. More than you would think, but it's nothing like having the voice.'

The voice, the self, the biographical interior. The desecration—was that the term Angie wanted?—of all Jane might fully be.

'Can she write?'

'Probably, but so far nothing doing. She holds the pencil, looks at it, puts it down. It's like she's saying there are no words for all of this anyway. It's like she's withholding. Mostly she stares at nothing, doesn't respond to questions with even the slightest hint of feeling. I've seen her scowl.'

'Scowl?'

'Like she's remembering something. But it doesn't last and doesn't bring her any closer to answering questions.'

'Can I meet her?'

'We'll see. No. Not yet. I'm guessing she'll end up in an institution of some kind, once she's physically well.'

And so the topic began to close.

'There's still media interest,' Bev added. 'You're not the only one out there searching for the story. I get calls every day, some offering "incentives" to talk.'

'I'm not "media interest", Bev. I'm not after a scoop or sensation.' Angie felt offended.

A wooden blind in the apartment began an irritating rattle. The wind was up, invasive; was it this windy last summer? They both ignored it, the wood-clack, the shudder, the way it knocked about in their troubled heads.

Then Bev gave in. 'For fuck's sake.' And she stood, wiped her fingers on a paper serviette and strode to the window. Pulled at the sash, lowered the pane. In an instant the sound was gone, the slats tightly closed.

Bev turned. 'Sorry, love. I didn't mean to lump you in with the bastards trying to get at our Jane.'

Our Jane. Bev too wanted to claim her. What was the nature of this irresistible attachment?

'Remember when we were kids, Ange, and we wanted to be noticed? To be the centre of attention?'

'More you than me.'

'Well, this is it, this is what it's like. A torrent of speculation, everyone wanting photographs, wanting access, wanting an interrogation. It sucks.'

Angie thought Bev was disingenuous. She'd been an officer most of her adult life and must surely have known what to expect: how a woman is intruded upon, how a woman is presumed known, and how what is unknown incites anger, or desire, or the wish crudely to expose.

'Don't get me started,' Bev added. 'The scumbags out there.'

Angie wanted to ask if anything had been discovered about Jane's ethnicity, but in the truce of their worry they turned to other topics of conversation. The weather was a reliably safe one to begin with. All this wind. The humidity. The disappointment of a damp, cloudy summer. Angie said she was walking more at night these days, sometimes quite late.

She saw Bev flash her policewoman's warning glance.

'You still swimming?' Angie asked.

'I haven't been back to the pool since I broke up with Lew.' Bev distracted herself by wiping the oil from the table. 'Coffee?'

'Still no word?'

'No, it's over. I think he's with someone else now, some saggy-arsed slut.'

'Bev…'

'Yeah, I know. Can't help it.' Bev changed the subject. 'You and Sam okay?'

Angie seesawed her hand to indicate so-so. Bev was the only one to whom she could be truthful, even when she said very little. Even when she hardly conceded the truth to herself. 'The thing is…' she began. But she did not finish her sentence.

Later, they shared the small blob of vanilla ice cream Bev discovered at the back of her freezer.

'Summer fun,' said Bev sadly. 'I owe you a decent meal.' She rose, continued clearing. 'All this wind.'

There was another sister.

A woman from Queensland rang Angie out of the blue to say she had been given this phone number if she wanted to talk. She wanted to talk. She knew Angie was a journalist; she just wanted to talk.

'How did you get this number?'

It was only then Angie learned that her phone number was circulating in independent support groups for those seeking officially Missing Persons. Perhaps Herb or Jake had publicised her number.

In the background to their phone call, Angie heard tropical birds. Summer in the north was wet too, and the wildlife was flourishing. She imagined wings of scarlet and green, and crested feathers uprising. A garish advertisement for spritz and soda, a bikini lady, sipping pink, and the turquoise rhomboid of a shiny, fern-shaded swimming pool, fresh with expensive light and erotic glitter. But it might have been a poor, dim apartment or a low-rent room.

The woman, who called herself Lisa, said that she had last heard from her sister one year ago, when Emily rang from Broken Hill. Lisa rambled a little, unsure how to begin. Then there was a raspy cough.

Poor, dim apartment, low-rent room. No trophy swimming pool.

'Then I heard "Broken Hill" in the report about the Unknown Woman, and thought, *Yes, it must be Em*. On the telly she didn't look like herself—but you'd expect that, wouldn't you, after a year of who knows what, apart from her family, stuck in a remote mining town. Em was always the adventurous one. Once, she sold her car and booked a flight to Fiji—Fiji, can you imagine!—and sent me a postcard. I felt pretty hurt she'd not taken me, but I was also mighty impressed. That's the kind of thing Em would do, blow all her cash, be a bit reckless, head off for no reason. Why Broken Hill I have no idea. A job maybe, something easy, something easy and unskilled.'

Angie let Lisa ramble on, unburdening.

'Em's four years older and I always looked up to her. She wanted to be a vet nurse but couldn't stand the study, so she did this and that, apprentice cook, checkout chick, helping at a garden centre. She drove our parents mad with not being able to stick to anything or settle down.'

Angie heard 'settle down' as if in italics. It was something people said. Jake/Abdul had said it too, as a crowning ambition. And she had told herself this about Sam: *Now I will settle down*.

'Anyway, I went to the police, of course. But nothing doing. They took one of those mouth swabs, the little cotton stick, easy-peasy, but no match. It took a while to sink in, that this Jane lady wasn't Em, but to be honest I knew it from the start. I knew Jane wasn't her. But it was exciting, just to open that possibility...'

And here Lisa paused to blow her nose, and Angie thought again of the grim toll of perseverance. No amount of wishing made things right.

'I have to say, the cops in Brisbane didn't really take me seriously. I accept it now, I guess. But the weird thing is that it hasn't stopped me thinking about her—Jane, I mean, and Em as well. It means Em's still out there, and I wonder if this Jane woman knew her, maybe they met in Broken Hill, and when Jane can speak she'll say, "There was this really cool chick, Em from Queensland, and she helped me all she could. And we had a friendship together. Hanging out. Having fun. And I know where she is."'

Silence then, as Lisa considered what she had just said. She might not have recognised the flimsy thread of her own hope until she announced it like this: that Jane held the secret, somehow, and would one day lead her to her dear lost sister.

'Well,' said Lisa. 'That's the story. Maybe you can help. Maybe you can keep my number and let me know if this Jane lady starts to talk. Maybe you can arrange a meeting. Or something else. Maybe?'

A further silence. This time Angie did not say, 'I am only a journalist, I cannot help you.' She said, 'Yes, I'll take your details in case there's anything to report.'

It was a lapse of judgement. She knew at once that it was a mistake, that she might have seeded a false trust, and that this woman in Queensland, this Lisa, grieving in her own way, strung out on rumours and possibilities, imagining any number of destinies for her larrikin sister, would now be waiting on the frailest of pretexts for her call.

As usual Sam had stayed in, mooching about, watching a crime show, shamefaced, then grading his students' papers. At the kitchen table, hunched like a tethered servant, he seemed defeated and unhappy. Angie went out, walking through the night.

In November the jacaranda bloomed; in December the jasmine and frangipani, the cape lilacs and the fig trees sprawled along the old streets. Now, in mid-March, there was the extra flourish of more rain. This lavish quality of her local world continued to delight her. Canopies shadowed the suburb with their leafy profusion, the road was glossed by streetlights, soft gleam issued in rectangles from quiet homes. The amplification of small sounds made her footfall noisy.

On this night she passed beneath the black domes of the fig trees beside the water and sat on the damp grass of the park to watch the boats moored on Blackwattle Bay. Small craft and large, all with whimsical names—*Windhover*, *Ruby*, *Henry's Delight*—and each moored above its own reflection, trembling in black mirror on the water. She liked the smell of these little bays, the dank properties of sodden undergrowth, the slime between the mangroves and on the wet side of the walls. Organic rot, and microscopic, teaming life. She liked the brackish water in the shallows that lipped in, and lipped in, seam after slow seam.

Calls and laughter. She turned.

She could just make out the name. On a boat called *Calliope*, anchored close in, there were four people drinking or sharing a boozy late supper. She saw their human shapes in silhouette. Mirthful and relaxed, their voices scrolled siren-like to the shore.

None of those Angie had interviewed thought Jane a mere shape. They all insisted she was known, and consequential. They shared a wish to refill the empty person with her hidden significance, to refuse heartless or slapdash lines of reportage. And the anxiety of the claimants was this precisely, that they believed they knew Jane but others did not, and so she risked being discarded or savagely renounced. A hood over a suspect, rough use by amateur assassins, whether by social media or a newspaper's nasty shout. We all strive to retain it, Angie thought, whatever muffled self is still there, distinctive and needful.

When they first met, Sam said that Angie tended to 'overthink'. It attracted him, her capacity for reflection, her constitutional seriousness. Now he found it tiresome, the way she wanted theories and explanations, the way she argued with him and held fast to her own position. She knew it; she knew he could not bear to be contradicted. She discovered obstinacy in herself, he discovered passivity, and as the years passed they fell into habitual compromise and denuded judgements. Neither had acknowledged this marital drift or foreseen its emotional consequence.

Far enough away, a couple were making out on a blanket on the grass; in the other direction a lone teen was fixed as a statue by his phone. Anzac Bridge stretched across the bay, with the dots of headlights moving along it, and beyond that the Harbour Bridge, neat and contained by distance. Her city, she told herself. This was now her city. But like many others, she had come from elsewhere. The world of her childhood meant that she retained a kind of country-girl wonder, that she would never take this for granted, or feel that she possessed it fully.

With a pang she wished she was with the revellers aboard the *Calliope*, drinking, talking, rocking on the water, faint and excited with the admixture of diesel fumes and champagne. Darkness hid their features, but they might invite her—who knows?—the woman alone, sitting at night on the shore. She might mingle, a half-invisible guest in their temporary company. It was less a fantasy of inclusion than of some mutual void.

And then the lightning started. Angie saw a crack in the sky and heard a low reverberation. An electrical storm was building in the muggy night. It was almost audible as a deep intake of breath. She felt great swishes of sudden wind and saw radiance glancing upon the water. Her thoughts flew away. The couple, now a smudge, were hastily gathering their blanket. The lone teen had left. A laugh rose from the boat as Angie clambered up the embankment, away from the bay, moving back towards home. She knew she was impractical, foolish, stupidly wilful, and that to be here now, in the rising squall, with light streaking and flaring, was an invitation to disaster. Still, she did not rush. The air was wild and magnetic with what locals called the Southerly Buster. There was noise too, unidentifiable, twangling instruments ringing in the air, and in the spin of wind she couldn't have said where the giddy sound came from.

Angie loved this, the astounding renewal of Sydney storms, the busting sky and the promise of boisterous torrents. And when the rain came it seemed altogether too much; it seemed to crash onto her. In no time gutters were overflowing with leaves and sailing rubbish; petals were spattering. One or two cars splashed past as she made her way, chilled and stumbling, overtaken by elation. Her route was a river now, and unclear. Her mind had rainfall inside it.

By the time she stood in her doorway, she was drenched and smiling like an idiot. Behind her, the hiss and moan of a wall of rain. She was wringing her clothes and hair, twisting her sopping shirt, stamping her squelching sneakers like a puddly child. Breathless, with the banging, lit sky above. Aware too of her predisposition to the melodrama of expanded feelings.

'A tempest,' she said to Sam. 'The isle is full of voices.'

He handed her a towel. '*Noises*,' he said. 'It's "the isle is full of noises".'

II

Bev rang to say they had a match. That Jane had been identified. 'Not much of a mystery, huh? Not much suspense, after all.'

Angie waited for more details but Bev was either distractedly busy or deliberately evasive. There were clattery office sounds, like washing dishes, and someone shouting in the background. Perhaps it was the question of, rather than the answer to, Jane's identity that had attracted her.

'Who is she?'

'Can't tell you just yet. We'll have a press conference after the parents fly in.'

Parents. Fly in. Like pigeons homing to their daughter. 'Give me a clue?'

'Just wait. You'll be invited to the press conference.'

Then more clatter, more shouting, and Bev hung up.

Angie sat back in her chair at the kitchen table. Her laptop was open. She wanted to take comfort in this news but something still troubled her. This was possibly the anti-climax that Sam had predicted. Yet it was also a 'result'—the nifty language of conclusion—and even though Jane was still unwell, a foundling gaunt and speechless, she would be returned to the arms of those who loved her. Those flying in. Their arms like wings outspread.

Angie ought to have felt some relief, but she brooded on what was left. The crime was still unsolved—that was it. There was still no knowing what had happened to the woman found in anonymous night. The woman dragged half-dead from a ditch at the side of the road. More pragmatically, more selfishly, Angie wondered if she'd lost her chance to meet her. Jane would now be even more protected from questions and the visits of inquisitive strangers.

Angie rose from her chair and walked outside into their tiny yard. Jasmine scent flowed there, and the whiff of a near neighbour's barbecue. Above, the bats were streaming east to west across the sky at the dusky end of day. She resisted seeing their shapes as somehow emblematic. Too easy to wax gothic, or to want symbols of portent readymade. The moon was rising and honed; the sky was ribbed with thin clouds; the cool of evening was a kind of vapour, softly descending. She liked them, the shapes, and whatever homing instinct the bats were aerobatically performing. They were smarter than pigeons, and certainly more spectacular.

And she liked too the delectation of wing-beat and lines of flight. To avoid serious thinking. To lift there, and move away.

What might the collective noun be? A wavelength of bats. Wavelength.

Under bright office lighting, the pall of glare and revelation, Angie stood in the crowd with the others. As usual, the key positions were occupied by television cameras and bulky men holding high their fluffy boom mics. Print journalists stood in solidarity behind and at the fringes. Two photographers were kneeling like seraphim, close to the raised dais, waiting for their money shot.

In the last week or two the story had gained traction abroad; the 'Oz horror' genre, always popular, had been invoked to give it spice, to decorate the tale of a speechless woman to whom terrible things may have happened. Outback barbarism was implicit, and the malevolent predation of women. Photographs of Broken Hill, empty-looking, parched, inhospitable, began to appear on media websites abroad. Gritty light. A surfeit of sun. The rotted poppet heads of mine sites. There was even a *New York Times* article: 'How Safe Is Australia?' As if crime didn't exist in the United States, or was so common there as to need a new location.

The internet was full of rumours, some grotesque. So when Detective Inspector Beverly Calder announced that the woman was a German national, there was a quiet moment and a few surprised and smothered whispers. Hannah Bloch—

the woman was Hannah Bloch.

Hannah Bloch was thirty years old and had been travelling solo in Australia, an adventure before she returned to Berlin to take up a postdoctoral fellowship. She had gone missing almost two years ago, and her parents had only recently heard of the Unknown Woman. They contacted their local *Polizei*, who connected to the case. A DNA match confirmed that Hannah was indeed their daughter, and Professor David and Sara Bloch flew to Australia to claim her. Yesterday, they had visited their daughter at the hospital in Sydney.

The first question, bizarrely, was: 'Is Jane speaking yet?'

No, Bev answered, *Hannah* was not yet able to speak to her parents. In turn, they asked for privacy at this difficult time. No, they would not be granting interviews to the press. No, nothing yet. They needed to spend time with their daughter and arrange her repatriation. They needed privacy, she stressed again. At some stage, the Blochs would make a statement, but they would not be taking questions.

Then someone asked: 'Is the DNA reliable?'

Bev was taken aback. She answered with neutral aplomb. 'The professional standards of our force are of the highest order. With international cooperation and the excellent forensic knowledge here in Australia, we have managed to establish and confirm beyond doubt the identity of Hannah Bloch.' She paused before adding, 'This is a good result.'

The assembled press were annoyed that the parents were not present. No dire camera feed, no useful photograph.

They'd been led to believe the parents would make a statement. There were one or two more questions in which Bev was asked directly if police had made further discoveries in the case. 'Any suspects?'

'Our investigation is ongoing. But a good result,' Bev repeated.

It was early evening, dusk approaching dark, and the friends walked in their jogging gear around the empty sports oval. The light rail rumbled nearby, elevated, screeching a little as it passed, and both glanced up to watch its slow, undeviating procession. Every train had this intrinsic charm, Angie thought. Any and every train. In its silver tube it carried the mixed cargo of office bods and daytrippers, of migrants and tourists, of students and construction workers, of shopping bags and strollers and small children who made a nuisance of themselves, standing on the seats with their precarious bodies, pressing their faces to the cold windows for a joyful peep. Any train.

'They know where they're going,' she quipped, and Bev responded with a grin.

Both had halted to watch the train, slowing motion, time heavy, as it crossed the bridge. The lit carriages swayed as they slid, and up there a child's face, as Angie had predicted, happy to be lofty, looking down on grown-ups, watching the world go by, and yes, offering the quick star of wave. Angie waved back. The child face flowed away, its brightness a pink blink, then gone.

'In training,' said Angie.

'A terminal case,' said Bev.

'Entrained, as surely as a body on a gym machine.'

'Yet the reigning of training stays mainly in methods of explaining.'

'Feigning training.'

'Ah, waning.'

'No-brainer training.'

'Deigning. Mere deigning training, no true reigning on Spaining…'

Angie conceded defeat. Bev always won these contests, in which they pointlessly riffed on any topic that attracted them.

The train continued on its way, to Lilyfield, to Dulwich Hill. Names colonial and quaint. It struck Angie then that skyscraper Sydney was Barangaroo, named as Indigenous. Names.

'Can I ask about Hannah Bloch?' Still merely a name.

'No. Too early.'

They continued their walk. The oval seemed the apposite shape for their non-progression. And Angie did not ask again about Hannah Bloch. She knew Bev well enough to change the subject, to enjoy the small pleasure of their walk, in which, this evening at least, even objects like trains were gliding by full of emanations, and the moon was floating upwards, breaching through clouds, and the water, as it grew darker, produced its own limp candles.

And after Bev waved goodbye, Angie thought: *Ah, the name. Regaining entertaining by Coltrane blue training.* John Coltrane's *Blue Train*, hard bop jazz, the saxophone notes returning as if they fell in a shower from the sky.

Now her mind was spinning out. Miles Davis playing improv for Louis Malle's *Elevator to the Gallows*, murder most foul. Ornette Coleman, Henry Threadgill, Charlie Parker, the saxophone greats. And the saxxy spiral of her own listening, and her own inner ear.

The cameras reassembled.

Only a few days later, the tired parents read a statement to the press. There were signs on their faces that they were distraught, that although their daughter was returned to them, she was terribly changed. They wore none of the pleasure of found life, but the collapsed look of the bereaved. Four police officers stood in a row behind them, guarding against further collapse. Unpersuasively, the uniforms recommended order.

The father read from a small card, while the mother stood rigid and silent by his side. They thanked the police in Australia. The people of Australia. They thanked Mr Terry Williams, who had been involved in Hannah's discovery. They thanked the hospital staff, naming one doctor and two nurses who had been particularly engaged with their daughter's care. Professor Bloch's German accent made his thanks sound especially formal.

The press release said David Bloch was a professor of biochemistry; Sarah had trained as a lawyer. They were middle-class professionals from Wilmersdorf, Berlin. And now, Angie thought, they were also strangely denationalised: it seemed an effect of this case, to remove nation and race, to remake bodies and faces in a peculiar obscurity.

The discovery of their daughter had not been a reclamation of family, but a confirmation of ubiquitous damage. Not unalloyed joy, or clear identity, but shadows of doubt falling over their faces.

Detective Inspector Beverly Calder stepped up to conclude the proceedings. She thanked her team and said that the wishes of all Australians were with the Blochs for a safe journey home and Hannah's full recovery. She said that there were over 2500 long-term—that is to say, for more than three months—officially registered Missing Persons in Australia. She reminded the public of the National DNA Program for Unidentified and Missing Persons, led ably by her colleagues in the Federal Police.

The photographers now had tokens of the tragically stricken. They filed their images of grief for one still living. They filed something meagre and something immense. It was clear too that there was journalistic disappointment: no tears of joy, no fainting mother, no spontaneous or personal disclosures.

Angie was thinking in self-interest: *I will never meet Hannah now. I will never even see her. There will be no opportunity to say, 'Speak, Hannah, speak. I am listening to your story. Speak.'*

Casually browsing on the internet, Angie located David and Sarah Bloch. David gave talks here and there and had published prestigious papers. Sarah Bloch had written a memoir of her family. Could it be the same Sarah Bloch? Bloch was a common name. There was an English translation: *Evermore Darkness.*

Angie ordered a copy online and waited to learn what darkness persisted. She felt an inciting and shameful wish to know, and even as the order went through she wondered at her hunger for this story. Something Marie said: a woman had appeared, not disappeared. And something else, too, bound by the same drive to recover: her own abiding sense that too much fell away, that life was too governed by disappearances, that any relic, even a glove, might return with tender relish the missing, beloved hand. That with little left, we were all gleaning, and obliged to hold fast what remained.

Lacrimarium: it was a beautiful word.

She was aware too that she had devised these forms of self-protection: antiquity, wordiness, artifice.

Evermore Darkness was authored by Hannah's mother. Her non-smiling photograph, postage-stamp size, was there on the back cover. The book was dedicated 'to my daughters, Hannah (Esther) and Rachel'.

So there were two children. And Hannah had a double name; why might that be so? Why was she also Esther? Was Esther a pet name, derived from early childhood: the occasional habit of small children to pick new names for themselves? (*Esta! Esta!* A child's urge for rebellion.) And there was a sister. A sister who must also have suffered after Hannah's disappearance, who must have watched day by day her parents' shared torment. She might have hidden her own misery in order to protect them. She might have tried to fill the space of two, to double her goodness and affection to cover the one missing. Or she might have withdrawn and become a second lost daughter.

Had she travelled to Australia to greet her found sister? Or had she been discouraged, dissuaded and afraid? Might she be, at this moment, alone and confused in Wilmersdorf, half-rejoicing, half-weeping, strung out on stories? Angie pictured a young woman with a face like very like Hannah's, but obstructed by her exclusion from the family drama, made crazed and disconsolate by her parents' travel across the planet. She felt sure they had left her behind to travel to scary Australia. Together and without her.

The cover of Sarah's book featured a huge night sky, above a mesh of barbed wire. Ah, as she'd suspected. Angie saw the subject now. She was not yet ready to read the history of Sarah and Hannah's darkened family.

Angie stored the book on her bookshelf in a line reserved for other unread books she had ordered on impulse, or for work, or bought because everyone else was reading them. The ominous title called out to her, but she walked away.

The bedroom door was ajar. Sam sat propped by pillows, reading a political thriller. Angie considered the light in the bedroom—one of those old-style dangling globes, from an austere and frugal era—was too diffuse to read by, but Sam persisted; he clearly had better eyesight than she. Angie resisted itemising the ways in which he was better or stronger, even though it might have allayed her critical mood.

Almost everything he did these days annoyed her: his mess in the bathroom, his trivialisation of her work, his wish to interrupt when finally she began to write. He considered her tastes ridiculously old-fashioned, and often, unkindly, could not resist telling her so. And he was correct, of course: black and white movies from Italy and France, boppy old pop songs, high-modernist novels, slow-durational, unwinding jazz; these misfitted Angie for what Sam like to call the real world.

Sometimes now he seemed furtive, like a man with something to hide. She half-hoped that Sam was having an affair, but to his credit, and unlike her, he was incapable of deception; or perhaps, given his passivity, he could not be bothered. That too—his passivity, his indifference to what engaged her, his suspicion that most emotions were hyperbolic and unbecoming. Their conjugal irritation was mutual, and both needed by some edifying alternative to be reminded of who they were.

'Any good?'

'The usual. Middle Eastern villains, stolen nukes, an American hero. There's a side plot with a transvestite who seems to be a master or mistress of disguise.'

'Transexual.'

'No, transvestite. Code-named Shirley Temple. I predict he's besotted with the hero. And will be sacrificed in a ball of fire.' He added, 'I totally see it,' as if echoing his students.

And this, his teen talk. His automatic authority. The air of amused lack of interest when she expressed an opinion. She thought of the expression 'come to grief', which her mother liked to use.

Sam resumed his reading and seemed immediately to forget Angie was in the room.

She undressed, tipped an old nightie over her head and slid in beside him. Sam shifted position slightly and tugged at the bedclothes. There was no chance tonight of sex or serious conversation. No chance either of witty or non-ironic exchange. The thriller, cynical in all aspects, had taken her husband far from complex feeling.

Angie tried an intervention. 'How come no one uses the word "gentle" anymore?'

Sam said, 'Mmm,' and turned the page.

So she turned too, to the wall, away from the glimpse of

a patch of grey hair on his chest that moved and aroused her, away from her own needs and his self-enclosure, away from what was intimate, what might cause embarrassment, what might require a different form of attention. A concession to vulnerability on both sides.

Then she heard, not saw, one finger and a page curled slowly to the next.

And as you read
the sea is turning its dark pages,
turning
its dark pages.

She loved this fragment of poetry: waves akin to turning pages. And vice versa, each page a wave. Some larger sense of correspondence and a poetical world. Recollection of these few words made her want to cry: their irrelevancy, their relevancy, and so very simple. The difference a line break makes. What a difference a day makes at line break. And the fact that she was composed of all this mixed-up cultural stuff: drifting phrases, lines from songs, literary quotations, rhymes and rhythms, scraps of image, nothing that really passed for coherent thought. Nothing that indicated a woman holding things together, holding a marriage together, and somehow coping.

She was sliding away from Sam now, into desires she couldn't yet name. Eventually he rose and turned off the light. She lay very still, pretending to sleep. Words were flipping in her head. Proper names, their syllables falling in her drowsy mind. Coltrane, Zagreb, Hannah.

And what was the sister's name again? Rachel. Rachel was the name of the sister.

Now she felt stranded. The story had fizzled. Angie walked the streets of her suburb at a somnambulist's pace, daydreaming a result. Result: the word had stuck. Later, she sat at the kitchen table, wondering if she should, or could, interview more forsaken and disappointed claimants. There was the model here of a contemporary predicament, of what fervent anticipation, then the dashing of hope, might sadly reveal. It resembled the psychology of quiz-show TV: the promise of an answer, or a prize, then the slap of disillusion when a smiling winner takes all. Or the momentum of desire, wanting its own completion, inspiring the contradicting feelings of abjection and wish for control. Or the artless equations of unrequited longing: misapprehension, obsession, the production of a distant ideal.

On a slatted wooden seat in Hyde Park, Angie was waiting for Bev, who had offered to buy her a drink and an early dinner to apologise for the pizza. It was a calm and luminous day: no hair-raising wind, no drizzle or damp. After the recent rains there were more-than-usual white ibises wandering on the grass, their bald heads bent, their black faces intent on worms, their scimitar beaks at the ready. Sydneysiders mocked them as 'bin chickens', but Angie liked fondly to ennoble them.

As a child she had loved Thoth, elegantly slim with his ibis head, and his bird face in profile. She had listed Egyptian gods as others did dinosaurs or footballers. She and Bev drew signs in the sand for each other, making a story of personal symbols. Angie had an image of herself lying on her back, lax and sleepy, reading beneath the pepper tree that stood in their yard; the shifting leaves, the country summertime, bronze and slow, the smell of sheep and ammonium phosphate in the drought-dusty air. No parents existed in this memory, no Bev, either, only absorption in her Egypt book and her own small hand, idly tracing a few hieroglyphic curves in the dirt.

A group of four boys in grammar school uniforms appeared from nowhere to lunge, with their satchels swinging. The ibises honked and scattered, but not before one was brutally hit and bowled over. In backward fall its wings opened; there was the squawk of a mad flap. For a while it lay quivering and prone, apparently unable to escape. Had its wing been broken?

Angie called, 'Hey!' and the boys turned in unison. She held up her phone and conspicuously filmed them. There was an indignant 'Fuck you!' and the middle finger; then the smallest boy, ashamed perhaps, or cowed by an imagined authority, shouted, 'Sorry, Miss,' as if she were a schoolteacher, reprimanding. One of the other boys hit him, open-handed but rough, on the back of his head.

The struck ibis found its feet and stood stunned, perfectly still. Like a bird that has flown smack-bang into a plate-glass window. She waited for it to toddle away, but impassively it stood.

Off they went, the boys, across the lawn and into the dense shade of the spreading figs, heading towards the bus stands on Elizabeth Street. The tallest, the one who hit, with gloating savagery and a laugh.

Angie approached and inspected the bird. It flinched its head in fear. She returned to her seat. The bird remained still. It seemed then to become an object and not to see her at all. There were other people now, heading home after school or work, crossing the park for a short cut, and the incident evaporated into peripheral and minor details—tomfoolery over there, mere boyish swagger, mucking around—and a train to catch in a hurry, or a bus.

Although they were now out of sight, Angie imagined the boys in their smart blazers waiting together at the bus stop, and she knew that they had already forgotten her. She saw them riding the bus to the wealthy suburbs, disembarking, entering the neo-something porticos of fancy homes, striding into a white kitchen, pulling open the fridge to down milk straight from the carton, as in an advertisement, wiping their sated mouths, widely smirking. And then she realised she was doing it again: categories, generalisation. She had no idea who these boys were, or what might lie beneath the scene in the park.

Calliope—where had she seen that name? The boat. The night of the storm. Calliope was a Greek goddess. Goddess of what? Her fallible memory: too much perforation. Losing even the gods.

Bev was late, as usual, and Angie waited with her one true virtue, patience. Small insects sprang parabolic in the summer air. The ibises returned in a cluster to what must have been their delicious spot, the hurt one now indistinguishable or gone. Slowly the city became manifest, the sounds and fumes of the traffic, heavy bus roar like the end of the world, the sense everywhere of din and agitated hurry. A woman fled by in a medical mask, then a second masked woman, head down. There were still a few masks about.

Angie felt rattled. During lockdown, the ibises reminded her of the plague doctors of historical Venice. Their beaky leather masks were shaped in an ibis curve, and the slits of their nostril holes were a fearful slash. The carnival masks, black-lacquered and tidied with a row of stiff lace, were no less sinister. Years ago, on a holiday, Sam had held one up to his face. It was a horrible transformation.

In her poor Italian she had said, '*No, niente maschere*,' and the shopkeeper, thinking her rejection a matter of taste, pointed to a pink mask, set with sparkles and bunches of ribbons. '*No, grazie, no.*'

She had always hated masks. Menacing things, even when comical, in their erasure of the human face. A devouring concealment. A doll disanimation. A clinical regularity. Most of the global population now hated masks.

Bev stood before her. 'What are you doing?'

'Free-associating. You?'

'Associating freely.'

And they hugged. Bev was in civvies, jeans and a floral shirt. In her police uniform, she was hyper-visible and looked large and important. Angie had always noticed how people around her, although presumably innocent, gave her guilty glances. Everyone seemed guilty. Bev could not be unaware of this effect of her uniform on others.

'First a bar, then Chinatown,' Bev announced.

'First Manhattan, then Berlin.'

'The monkey and the plywood violin.'

'Enough already,' said Angie, 'as they say in Nu Joisy.'

Their banter enlivened them. Bev was relaxing and Angie could almost hear the Leonard Cohen song playing its verses in her head. At the bar they sat side by side on high brass stools. Bathed in the glow of sepia lights sparking off a row of hanging wine glasses, Bev listened to Angie's story about the boys in the park, and the injured bird. Not much of a crime, in her books. But she pretended to care, Angie thought. She actually listened, and predictably she asked, 'Did you get a photo?' This had been her advice for years: if something disturbs you, take a photograph. But discreetly, without being noticed.

'You know they're not Egyptian,' Bev added.

'Yes, you know that I know.'

Some used the epithet 'sacred' to import the glamour of

Egypt into Australia. When she'd first arrived, Angie had taken photographs and tagged them 'sacred ibis'. And of course, they were. She grew to an adult before she understood that everything here, in this country, was sacred—creatures, rocks, land, sky, all precious with story, all stretching to deep time, all known in wise dimensions of ritual and song.

Her child-invented Egypt still returned when she saw the Sydney ibis. Beyond derision lay those early drawings, her glyphs and friezes, her made-up mythologies. She wanted pure bird, pre-colonial, pre-garbage and full of grace.

'Two names?'

'Yes, two. Hannah and Esther.'

'The passport says Hannah. I've seen it.'

'Did you recover the passport?'

'No, of course not. The digital. Courtesy of the *Polizei*.'

There were flower-shaped dim sum in round bamboo dishes, small saucers of condiments, a whole fish, a barramundi, covered in chilies and ginger, a tub of rice, and a pretty plate, blue and white, of wilted green leaves. They were the only non-Chinese customers in the restaurant and both enjoyed the novelty of their seeming displacement. Other patrons ignored them and ordered with more confidence. Under vermilion lanterns and double-happiness signs, a child-sized woman circulated, proffering an enormous teapot. There was stuffy, food-scented air, and the comforting sound of laughter from the nearest table.

'Consider the debt paid,' Angie said. 'My turn next. Sam would like to see you; perhaps you could join us? Make a time?'

And only then Bev told her, speaking cop shorthand. She was to be seconded to Broken Hill for a couple of months, to lead the investigation there. Little progress had been made; the case could not yet be closed; no clear result; noises from 'upstairs', complaining; the usual; et cetera, et cetera. 'You'll have to visit or I'll go mad from booze and loneliness.'

Yes, she would visit. And here Angie saw another story opening before her, and time away—necessary time away, perhaps—from Sam, and respite from whatever was happening between them.

'Lack of resources,' Bev went on. 'And I'm the lead on the case. Upstairs wants results.'

That word again.

Bev was tucking into the barramundi. She was a devil with chopsticks.

'Why couldn't the secondment have been to somewhere like Hawaii?'

'Next time,' said Bev.

On her walk home around the harbour, Angie thought she might visit the bays. She wandered through Barangaroo

Reserve, keeping a good distance from the skyscrapers on her left. Then she slipped the peninsula to miss Pyrmont Bay, Jones Bay and Johnstons Bay and headed instead directly across to Blackwattle Bay, then along the park's edge towards Rozelle Bay.

There were one or two late-night joggers, fanatically calculating their steps, but it was mostly quiet, with almost no one on the harbour tracks. Light flashed on the water and Anzac Bridge hummed with its winking, night-time cars. Tired now, she cut through Bicentennial Park, then uphill, pushing and puffing into the dim streets. The walk had dissipated some of her nervous energy, but she was still improvising her feelings, wondering whether prematurely she had entered a midlife crisis, to be so without purpose and so pathetically contingent.

It was bin night and the green and yellow plastic bins were lined as requested on the footpath before each house. Sentinels, monoliths, the blocky, obedient shapes of an ordered suburban life. Angie stood still on the slight rise at the top of her street, took a deep breath and clasped her hands behind her neck, considering. She could knock over all the bins, even set up a domino effect of spillage; or she could run as if in a tackle and knock a few sideways; or she could make a rebel yell or shout a nineties song. On the main road, just out of sight, a wailing ambulance passed by. Not far behind came the sound of a police car, or two. She was adjacent to an emergency, she thought, *adjacent*. Had she drunk too much with Bev? Had she lost her senses? The bins stood sombre and dull in the inadequate streetlighting, no longer of interest.

Angie turned into her street and walked slowly down the hill. The siren sounds had retreated. It was late, she realised, and Sam would be in bed. He might be asleep. He might be restfully dreaming or grinding his teeth with resentment.

As they shared breakfast, a spider the size of a baby's hand plopped from above and walked its eight articulate limbs across the kitchen table. A huntsman: ash-grey, with banded legs and eyes like tiny black pearls. It must have fallen from the ceiling, where, Angie suspected, there was a crack to the darkness of a thriving nest.

Sam left the room. Angie did the drinking glass and paper trick, putting her broadest glass over the spider, careful not to catch the legs until they retracted, then sliding a stiff piece of paper below, so the spider could be safely transported. It crouched in its glass cage, ready to spring. Carefully she manoeuvred her way outside and flung the spider into the passionfruit vine that straggled along the back fence.

'Safe now,' she called to Sam, and he reappeared, abashed. Pest control was one of their many topics of argument.

Sam was blotched pink with waning fear. Angie did not mention the spider removal. So they continued telling each other about their separate yesterdays. Sam, quieter now, was drained of his early-morning belligerence. When he'd emerged from the shower, steaming, he might have been ready for a fight; he looked positively gladiatorial with his bare chest and towel. Now he half-listened as Angie told him about the boys and the ibis, and the fine dinner with Bev.

'We should go there sometime,' she added, even though he favoured Italian. And in order not to mention Broken Hill.

This was middle-class life, Angie told herself, holding on to fellow feeling in weary small details, sharing gripes, observations, offering a prospect of dining pleasure. Grand and significant things happened in another world.

In truth, she owed Sam an explanation but had none to give. She had not rung to say that she would be late. She had gone AWOL, he said. And he was correct: she had not asked his leave and had been absent without it. In the sunshiny clarity of a new day, she was aware of the army metaphor, taken perhaps from his thriller, used to describe her delinquency. He'd said it twice: AWOL.

Angie poured more coffee for Sam. But without drinking it he turned, seized the car keys and made for the door. 'First rehearsal,' he called back, and she remembered that he was directing the school play, *Hamlet*. Killing two birds with one stone, he had told her.

And slowly, deploring waste, Angie drank Sam's coffee.

She really should have rung him. She detested all forms of passive-aggressive behaviour. Her fault. He might have been worried sick. Pacing the room. Scanning his phone. Or perhaps he had enjoyed his thriller, and only when he was tired had she vaguely flitted into his head—*Not back yet, dining with Bev.* He'd have gone to the toilet, turned out the light and then found in narrative remnant, on the very edge of sleep, the dismissive label *AWOL*.

After she heard him drive away, Angie stood at the kitchen sink, without the will to do the breakfast dishes. Over-caffeinated and twitchy, she instead swept the floor. A second spider scurried away, climbing the wall. She decided to ignore it.

Then there occurred one of those moments in which a woman in a house stands in silence looking out the window. She thought of it like this, an old-fashioned, cinematic posture, a general air of discouragement, stopped action, lethargy, loneliness. A bird might pass by, a dog next door might bark. Yet all felt, nevertheless, remarkably still. The elements of an ordinary day seemed suddenly to insist on decipherment, as if they were a code intended solely for her, a code of what might change or remain the same. There was a sense of human arrest, with the non-human world continuing.

Calmly, not raddled, she wondered at what point other women decided to leave. At what point in a marriage was something irrevocable said, known or done?

Outside, soft light was filling the courtyard. The passionfruit vine was past fruiting but still greenly lush and assertive. A noisy myna bird was hopping there, buoyant with life. No wind. A clear morning. The lemon radiance of the early hours.

Angie returned to her tidying-up. Sam was a good man.

He was not abusive or violent, but far, far away. They still teased each other and spoke with affection. But both would have struggled to define what it was they now had in common. Theirs was a marriage within which each had abridged themselves.

She turned the tap and did the dishes, placing their plates in a line on the sink. Every marital interior was a secret one. The sympathies within it. The turmoils. The chastening effect of so much closeness. And the essential enlargements. In the beginning she knew his love conferred a particular joy, which she reciprocated. But some stifling habits had emerged, and a tone of casual accusation for vague trespasses or mistakes. Tepid reproach. Fake contrition. Careless but hurtful resentment. Once he had argued for twenty minutes over her decision to stay with her mother, who was unwell. A few days, only a few days. He had wanted compliance and presence, even if it was heavy with his demand and her determined refusal.

It was lighter outside now: how she loved the brightness. She found herself gulping at the air of this unusual summer. It was sweet air, and humid, and scented with flowers inevitably white, and she noticed her sense of disturbance abating, becoming something else, returning her to an adjusted, necessary calm. This too, their shared tendency to skid away from difficult feelings.

Involuntarily—ready now—she thought of her project, and decided it was time to return to her work. Angie took *Evermore Darkness* from her unread shelf. It was a hardback, loaded with history. She opened at random and saw 'Treblinka', 'my mother'. Sarah Bloch's mother's name had been Else Ausländer. Else, Sarah, Hannah (Esther), Rachel.

Angie closed the book. This was still not the right time. Or she was not yet ready to intrude—since that was how it felt—into the backstory of a family in newly discovered ruin. A sense of hesitation, even prohibition, overtook her. She was losing her nerve.

The photograph of Sarah Bloch on the jacket of the book was formally elusive. Angie saw it now, in the set of the face, in the direct stare at the camera, the way that her fortitude had been earned by imagining her mother on the rim of an abyss, Else Ausländer as a young girl confronting the knowledge that night had invaded, that everything—everything—might soon come to an end. A young girl seen by others as a category, with her future gone.

The pause was instructive. Angie held the book in her hands. There was more to think of than whether to resume or leave her marriage, or whether to lie in bed face-to-face or turned away. She was reminded of a wider scale and other meridians, those lines of story, beyond her own, that included extremity, danger and the histories of nations. The weight of knowledge for which bleak night hours were only the vaguest approximation.

During the next month, the weather in Sydney calmed. The crackle in the air shifted register, the slanted rain discontinued, the sky opened more spaciously, fair and temperate. Angie and Sam agreed that they would try harder to reconnect. They were careful with each other and spoke in a soft, almost melancholy tone that carried the hint of erotic longing. They touched each other's forearms or brushed an invisible fleck from a shoulder. They kissed on parting. They slowed a little, shifting the pace of their conversation, mindful of inflection, nuance and tone.

Mellowed by such practices, they found their bodies again, the drive of attraction, and the fun of it, and the simplification. She'd not forgotten this, the waver of mixed breath, him taking shape inside her, the way the night in awesome darkness seemed to shake and fall open. In the lassitude afterwards, they joked as they subsided, as each removed strands of the other's hair from their new-felt mouths.

Morning came as if they lived in the country. City noises receded. Light recovered promise. They heard birdsong, delivered as a lyric poem.

Angie had declared that in a few weeks she would visit Bev in Broken Hill, and this gave them the calendar of their renewal. Sam seemed pleased with the modesty and limit of her suggestion. It depressurised and bracketed the real issues in their marriage.

In the meantime, each practised their work with restored dedication. Sam had found something at school he'd not known was there. When students read aloud in class, they expressed grievance, they were plodding and indignant, lugging the old-fashioned words. But on stage, he said, given a cardboard sword and new name and a licence to overact, they conveyed an unanticipated pleasure, and he had found the spark of teaching again. In class they answered him in a manner that implied coercion, their adolescent tongues twisting un-Shakespearian, but in their rehearsals they'd spoken differently—they'd discovered new qualities in themselves.

The detection of Jane's identity had not wholly discouraged claimants. Angie continued to take calls and collected voices in her phone. This was purpose enough, she told herself, it was an honourable gathering of stray and neglected feelings: mocked convictions, theatrical need, implacable desire, genuine grief. She was producing not a crime story but something broader: acknowledgement of that which spun invisibly, like a force field, around any crime. There were chat groups out there, and organised searchers, and they passed her name between them as an interested journalist who might be able to help. The vast range of losses, solemnities, crazy projections—she respected them, and somehow the claimants had known it.

Angie was not habitually rationalist, nor an opponent of fuzzy sentiment, so she was empathetically susceptible to the wide range of appeals. But still she said, 'No, I cannot help you,

I'm just a journalist, researching a story, not even employed, a freelancer.' And still no one quite believed her.

From time to time Bev rang from Broken Hill, usually to complain. She spoke of her sense of isolation and her frustration with the local police. Angie looked up her workplace, an old building that resembled a pub. Made of colonial brick and stone, it had two levels, with an arched walkway and a covered veranda running along the upper storey. But for the blue and white checks on the flagpole and the ER badge set into the brickwork, it could easily have been yet another pub.

They didn't like outsiders, Bev said. A few were hostile and suspicious. Some backtalk, some conniving and low, hissing whispers. A cigarette butt in her coffee. A penis drawn on her notepad. Snide and terse misogyny. So she spent her time away from work reading or watching TV; she ate alone, drank alone, longed for Lew. Angie repeated that she'd given a commitment to Sam that she would stay in Sydney for the next month, but she would visit after that, if Bev was still there, and then they would properly talk.

Bev felt unable to disclose too much on the phone. 'Fill you in later.' But in her usual style, refusing at first to speak but then confiding a little in her friend, she gradually informed Angie that they were searching for a place where Hannah might have been held. Without giving details, she said that they were examining old mine sites around Silverton, twenty-six kilometres north-west of Broken Hill, a shithole mining town, she said, barely even that, barely even a shithole, with a population of fifty, or forty-four, or forty-eight people. No one was really sure, but it was pretty damn small. Known principally for its *Mad Max 2* museum. 'I'll take you there, you'll love it,' Bev added with no conviction.

Angie felt sorry for her. She sounded distant and stranded.

The internet said that Silverton was a 1176-kilometre drive west from Sydney in the desert outback. It was the location of film sets, lead mines, silver and zinc. It was surrounded by the rust-coloured and Instagram-friendly Mundi Mundi Plains, much depicted from the sky in feature films, captured by high sweeping drones that showed, in Bev's words, how distance remade a shithole into a sun-drenched glory.

Sam found again the cradle of her arms, made himself comfy against her breasts. They laughed in bed. There was this, at least, their physical comfort. One night he fell back smiling and announced his secret ambition. He'd realised he could be a director, he said, maybe youth theatre. He had a knack of releasing something special, he went on. Rehearsals had been going for only a few weeks, and though he'd never directed before he felt immediately confident in the role.

'The kids love disguising their voices in the lines of others,' he said. 'They all think they're celebrities, or might be, and it makes them bold. They project into the school hall as if they're starring in the West End. The parents are pleased too. Always classy, Mr Shakespeare.' Sam wore the exultant expression of one who knew his true vocation.

Angie lay on her back, listening to the spirited maunder of Sam's new version of himself. It was touching, his wish to connect with young people, his sense that acting did this, made its own kinship of expression, enjoined others in temporary but vigorous community. Her lonely lost speakers were at the other end of performance, hushed by their unhappiness, tentative in her company, assuming authority only in their most private and dreadful knowledge of loss.

Sam was now thinking of his actors. 'Imagine *Hamlet* in face masks,' he said, 'to show what we've all been through. So relatable.'

'No,' Angie said. 'No masks. *Niente maschere*.'

Sam looked puzzled. 'What?' His tone had shifted. She heard in the single word something disappointed and wary.

It was her memory, of course, not his. Not shared. He had no idea what she was referring to. No Venetian masks returned to him, no budget holiday in a one-star pensione in Mestre, living daily on bread and cheese and plastic flagons of red wine bought from the jolly man waiting in an enclave somewhere near the old ship-building area. No plague doctors, ibis-like, nor Carnivale, with its strident, demanding, fiercely drunken celebration. Tourists falling into the canals, bad behaviour, photographed excess. With a shock she realised that this was almost fifteen years ago. Now they might have been communicating by satellite, hemispheres apart.

It was a small matter, but it upset her. Could she have said why? Why, in any case, should he remember their talk about the masks? An irksome subject. It was no great mistake, no actual disloyalty. Was it George Eliot who said that marriage was a special mode of inattention? Or was it attention? Angie rose from the bed, aware of her own body and movement. The headlights of his stare, his ignorance of her sadness. She moved to the doorway and switched off the light, needing to hide in the dark, to recover her own face, and her own sense of self.

It was a Saturday morning. Sam had invited some of his drama students to an extra rehearsal, a 'workshop', he called it, in their too-small house. It was beyond school rules to have them visit, but they were keen, he added, and willing to give up a few hours of their weekend. Hamlet and Horatio were there, as well as Gertrude and Ophelia. No King Claudius or Laertes, no Polonius lurking, and none of the minor characters.

Angie thought Hamlet an exceptionally handsome boy and wondered, since he was dark and un-Danish, if he'd been chosen for his against-type good looks. Ophelia was pretty—Sam might have had a weakness for simpering blondes, narrow and sweet—but Gertrude was magnificent. A large girl, Lebanese perhaps, and full of actressy ardour and womanly swagger. It was hard to believe she was only sixteen; she would certainly steal every scene in which she performed. Horatio wore a hoodie, even though it was warm; this was clearly his style and nothing would persuade him to relinquish it.

Later, she asked Sam if Horatio planned to wear his hoodie onstage. 'Maybe,' he responded, in a tone that said *modern interpretation*.

Angie headed out to buy the papers and a bag of croissants for Sam's guests. Everyone outdoors, it seemed, was dragged by a lively dog, or coaxing a child with a scooter to behave. The latest must-haves: a scooter and a dog. A scooter, a child and a dog. A scooter, a child and a designer dog. She would never fit in.

The weekly market in the school grounds was already abuzz, but a brief speckle of raindrops sent Angie heading into the bookshop on the opposite side of the road. Her temple, Sam liked to joke. Here, indeed, she became reverentially solemn. She moved slowly around the neat terraces of the new releases, wrapped in whatever yearning the words and images directed at her. She was this woman too, compelled by the gist and promise of a title, moved by the hope of self-clarification. There were dozens of books she wanted not just to read but to own, to claim the worlds pressed effectually between their covers. It was a kind of thrall, this something that came into being with the charm of another mind. Or an escape hatch, a squeezed passage into disguise and the release of not being herself.

Other readers browsed too, serious types and students and what is sometimes called the 'general public', all roaming solipsistic in the wend of a personal search.

Angie purchased a novel but knew she would hide it, to avoid Sam saying yet again that she had too many books, that she was a sucker of late capitalism and the dupe of populist industry.

On the pavement just outside the bookstore, a young man was begging for coins. His paper cup jiggled. He was ragged and unshaven and had the stench and crumple of sleeping rough. And the listless quality those who live on the street seem to acquire. He recognised Angie as a patron: 'Morning, miss!' Too chipper, too familiar, so that she was obliged to notice, and to pay. In their small drama he was Fate and she was Agency, and as his hands scooped at the air, ready for money, she wanted her own concealment and not to register his face.

Angie opened the front door as Sam was telling his performers that Hamlet was a student, that these were students' ideas—love, conflicts with parents, thinking you've seen a ghost. 'Acting out,' she heard as she walked through to the kitchen. She made coffee in a large pot and they gathered around the table.

Angie called out: 'No Danish pastries, I'm afraid. No Danish here!'

No one got the joke and Sam shot her a look of pity. It

was true what he said—she didn't know how to talk to young people.

The rain had been the thinnest dash of a shower, but every leaf and every paving stone had taken on a lacquer of shine. Passionfruit and jasmine both appeared unearthly. There was a racket of currawongs from the large trees across the back laneway, and the sound of cockatoos cackling further afield as they shredded a palm. It was a good summer for the birds.

Angie dragged a chair out into the damp courtyard and read the Saturday papers, half-listening while the small cast practised their lines, Sam filling the roles of all those absent. The style of speech was declarative, and the script had been drastically edited. Many of the speeches were less than half their original length, and some had a few contemporary lines or references spliced in. She guessed that whole scenes had been redacted. *A Seriously Condensed Hamlet. Hamlet Made Easy. Hamlet for Student Beginners.*

Angie would say nothing to Sam but she was a purist in this regard: she hated the thought of a mutilated text. She hated the bard being treated like a sozzled old geezer, who needed to be sat down in a corner, quietly disposed of, to give way to the young folk with their pool cues and their hoodies.

Later, they would know this as the period of calm before everything collapsed.

Angie had bought her train ticket and was looking forward to Broken Hill. Two days before she was to leave, Sam received a phone call early in the evening. He stiffened and his hand fell to his side as the talking continued.

Angie assumed it was his father, Mack—his heart condition and his tenuous grasp on life. She'd sometimes imagined old Mack, after two heart attacks, keeling over, still clutching his bent cigarette and his fat tumbler of whisky. A bloke from the old school, proudly neglectful of his health. 'Good enough for my dad, good enough for me,' he liked to say. But within seconds something told her it was not Mack at all.

And then Sam slumped, pale and buckled, into the lap of the couch. 'Robbie De Soto,' he said. 'My student. My Hamlet.'

Sam's body was slack now, and smaller. He was shrinking into himself. He didn't cry, or say anything more to Angie, but blinked at her, infant-like, as if inquiring what he should do next. And then at last he asked, 'Should I ring the parents with my condolences? Should I arrange the service? Or a notice? Or flowers for the stage in the hall?'

It was a disordered ramble. None of this would be Sam's duty to organise.

'I feel somehow responsible,' he said quietly, as if he'd read her thoughts.

Robbie De Soto, beautiful Robbie De Soto, dark, handsome, chosen as Hamlet, and in the distracted globe of his mind he had chosen not to be. The world was weary, stale, flat and unprofitable. Just over a week ago this Hamlet had sat at her kitchen table, solid and deceptively permanent, his gaze shyly averted, pressing at flakes of pastry with his index finger.

At funerals Angie had seen the bereaved mumble, and nod, and grasp at one another's hands. She had seen vague stares and the reaching out for a close embrace. She had seen sore spots exposed, like bruises, and others summoned to help. But speaking of Robbie, Sam did none of this, nothing needy: he was blank and separate. When he addressed her it was in a tone of defensive petulance.

Under cover of darkness, in bed, Sam told her he'd decided to make a feature of the soliloquy, so that everyone who knew the line—'to be, or not to be'—would take it seriously.

'Take it seriously,' he'd told Robbie. 'This dude wants to top himself.'

He was a teacher talking hip, acting as a friend, like mates gaming side by side, or half out of it, smoking weed together on the weekend. Sam prided himself on what he'd been able to say during the rehearsals, how his role had made him popular, how the other teachers had noticed. Now he was confiding in his wife. He was saying: *It's my fault. Mine.* 'Top himself. I said that.' There was a lack of conviction in his tone.

Angie thought of Ophelia—what did he say to her? Top herself? But she stayed silent, contained these unspeakable fears, worried in secret that his wish for admiration had made him foolishly bluster, reckless with others' lives. They were smirched by this, by this beautiful boy destroyed. This boy who had sat vivid, fully alive, at their kitchen table.

Sam was troubled in a way that she couldn't reach and didn't know how to answer.

In the morning, unnerved, he called in sick. The rehearsals would of course be cancelled, and with them, in Sam's view, his own possibility to be another kind of man. His sense of ambition had closed before it had fully opened.

'Just a boy, only sixteen, with his whole life ahead of him,' Sam said.

He knew these phrases but spoke dutifully, without apparent feeling. A colleague rang to say that Robbie's parents and younger sister were demolished by their grief. *Demolished.* The headmaster wanted to speak to him. Could he write a tribute? Could he locate a Shakespearian quote to print for the funeral service? Could he ring the school office as soon as possible? Could he come in, immediately?

In shock, cowardly perhaps, Sam arranged a medical certificate that covered him for a week's leave from work. 'It's just like a movie,' he went on, and for a moment she hated him. Such a fatuous comment. There was no remorse here, but something else: regression to self-interest. Sam sounded heartless and hollow. Turning away, he had seen only his own face.

When Angie came into the living room later that morning, she saw Sam blearily lost. He was bent over his phone, seeking news anywhere, in any stream, on the death of his student. He found nothing—too early, perhaps. News threads do not report such minor matters, unless of course Sam was to be blamed in a public way or called publicly to account for something he had said or done. Social media might hound him; other students, in their own grief, might turn against him, with good reason or with no good reason. He looked up and shrugged, exasperated.

Angie thought of the boy's younger sister—how she had coped, or not. She rang Bev, who listened. 'He said it was just like a movie.'

Bev heard her tone. 'People say that kind of thing when they hear bad news.' She paused before naming it. 'When they feel guilty. Or overwhelmed.'

Angie was unable to respond.

'Don't judge him, Ange. Don't hold it against him.'

The counsel was sound. She should not have judged him. She had thought him a dissembler, and too fond of cliché, when she should have practised compassion.

'Couples disappoint each other all the time,' Bev continued. 'All the time. We get on with it. We keep trying.'

Now Bev, once again, had said too much. Both somehow knew it. Bev's investment in their marriage now felt tactless and prurient. Angie was sorry that she'd rung. She wanted time alone. She wanted silence, and to think about something else.

One of the later claimants, a man called Alex, said that his sister had left for her tennis lesson at the age of ten and never returned. He was then twelve. She was dressed all in white and swung her racquet as she left. He had no idea what she would look like now, his Lil, but he dreamt about her from time to time, always in her tennis whites, always walking away, swallowed by tree-shadow, by distance, by a mauve-toned mist he thought of as a kind of *presentiment*. 'Is that the right word?' he had asked.

'Yes, that's the right word.'

She was always ten years old. 'It's fixed,' Alex had said. This memory of her, just a few seconds, really, in her short white tennis dress. 'It's there in my memory and it's there in my dreams. Just a few seconds.'

Alex's voice had trailed off and Angie knew he was thinking of Lil again, his sister stylised and skewed in the moment of her disappearance. The sister in mauve mist may have been a tormenting recurrence, or it may now, with the lapse of time, have become a salve, a comfort.

'My mother managed,' he said. 'Threw herself into religion and charity work, filled up her empty time. But my poor father fell into a heap. He stopped working, stopped living, sat on the veranda for hours, expressionless and somehow resigned to the power of the stopped world.'

The snow man again, hidden in this disclosure.

For a short time Angie had closed her eyes. Her phone was recording a protracted silence.

There was no honour in her retention of this fleeting image, the man and the ruined house with the dead family inside it, no point in making a glimpse into a fetish, in wanting to find an existential principle or an explanatory logic. There was no principle or logic. And it was not Angie's loss anyway, but someone else's, a kind of emotional theft from another country, with other customs and other languages. Was this how despair began, the incorporation of others' experience as one's own, the loss of any moral and national scale? On television there were many similar scenes of disaster. There was no reason to install this man as a significant fixture, like a worshipful figurine on a platform in a scarlet temple, wreathed by fuggy incense rising in slow curls. Yet still he remained.

And this, she thought too, was a kind of education: learning what falls away and what remains, contemplating why she was attracted to these images and what they held for her, and whether something in her wish to make an artefact of feelings might be, after all, her own futile search, unwisely elaborated, for something long gone.

And Sam had not been impervious, or hardened, or unaware of his role.

She came in with the shopping, placed her heavy bags on the kitchen table and heard his voice in the courtyard, voluble and wrecked.

She was struck by his posture. He was kneeling, head down, seeming to hold and examine himself like a man who had injured his hand. Or bent like a rower before the act of rising to exert a direction. Or like a penitent, beseeching, and making his body small. It had taken a week, but now, in their little space, he was crouched and crying.

She went to him, then. 'Oh, Sam.'

He seemed at first to resist, then submitted to her embrace. As she squatted to clasp him, he began to quake and, in a low, broken voice, to wail. 'What have I done, Ange? What have I done?'

It was inside him now, culpability, and the knowledge that something would never be repaired. How she loved him at that moment, now that he conceded damage, and was small.

III

The journey was long. Angie sat in the train, economy class, for the fourteen hours it took from Sydney to Broken Hill. There were no sleeping compartments, but rigid chairs, and meal breaks perpetual, during which the carriage filled with the cloying, childhood smell of hot pies and sausage rolls. Beer, wine and soft drinks were sold at inflated prices. The train, she read, was built in 1993, and in a time-warp sensation the ambience was also 1993. Jokey staff. No wifi. Sweet biscuits in natty cellophane and a teabag in a paper cup. A sense of simpler times, less provisional, more artificially solid. Yet she loved it, the entrained movement, the glide through the Blue Mountains and down to the tablelands and grasslands, then onwards to farms and towns given scale only by curving roads and faraway trucks.

A spray of black crows shot from silos and steel containers near the station at Parkes, and from then on the small towns disappeared. The scrubby plains unrolled; vast, lazy, flat lands of spinifex and saltbush extended in all directions. In the arid zone, beyond farms, lively creatures came into view: grey kangaroos dumbly standing, heads turned in a posture of unconcern, packs of feral goats made silly with the rumble of train noise, emus flustered and gawky, fanning agitated and rocking away into the hazy distance. The train was a wedge, pushing steadily at a soft, fleeting world. Then the land emptied to deep red and a distant, high blue, and those who bothered to gaze out the window might have recalled an Indigenous painting, the thousand dots of low spinifex and a necessary quality of abstraction. Towards the end, a speccy sunset, and further still it came at last, the starry and fast-falling night. Apart from the glimpses of animals, the journey might have been an allegory of non-event, of the outer world disengaged, disinterested and simply flowing by.

Every now and then Angie had risen to stretch her legs and to walk the short length of the train, and what struck her were how many passengers were deeply asleep, safe now, being taken, free of any decisions for fourteen hours. They gave themselves over to inactivity, train hum and predictable rest. Angie felt tender towards the sleeping souls, most, by the look of them, country folk, with two conspicuous tourists, a young Japanese couple pressed at the window, appreciative, exclaiming and taking photographs with their phones. *Kangaroo! Kangaroo!*

The train arrived in darkness. Bev was waiting on the brightly lit platform to meet her. She appeared unhealthy. She was sallow and glum. Angie was relieved to see she was in civvies and could have been mistaken for a local. Bev waved hello and made a swift grab for her wheelie case as they embraced.

'You must be starving,' she said, and headed off, no nonsense, leading the way to the car park. Behind them was a monumental waste dump, looming and gloomy, so close as to seem a pressuring threat against the railway.

'The pride,' said Bev, 'of Broken Hill. See the labour, see the mountain of hardened black waste.'

They would need wine, Angie decided.

The restaurant proclaimed 'European cuisine' and listed spaghetti, steak, spanakopita and schnitzel. Seafood basket. Side salads. Sweets. Angie skimmed the menu and said, '*Wednesday! Schnitzel!*' and yes, Bev smiled.

'Food starting with S has a special appeal here,' she responded. 'But where is the snake? Where is the shrimp? Where is the saltimbocca?'

Both ordered the spanakopita, playing it safe, enjoying the pararhyme. 'With shiraz,' Angie added, as she requested a bottle from the young man in the black T-shirt, who, they agreed, took their order both sweetly and sardonically.

A photographic print of the Swiss Alps hung beside them, with the tiny red-and-white flag and a Tourist Authority stamp. White-capped peaks, menacing.

'Country style,' said Bev. 'Service slow, décor execrable, food aspirational.'

They would each revive in the other's company. This friendship was reliable in its tolerance of bad jokes and convivial dining in any degree of good or bad taste. Before long they entered into the absorption of each other's world. Angie described the distended calm of the train ride—Bev had taken the plane, a mere two and a half hours—and tried to evoke the sense of a spacious loss of self, the pleasure of gliding, the way in which, just gazing out the window, she had entered an altered consciousness, not unlike the euphoria after lovemaking, with its combination of daze, exultation and deep, sensual rest.

'Gawd, what a romantic. You didn't mention the nonstop talker, the shrieking infant, the mum at the end of her tether.'

'That too.' (The rueful grimace-smile of a young mother exhausted.)

'The soapy cheese in its plastic envelope impossible to open.'

'That too.' Angie had been trying to amuse her friend by these flights of fancy.

Bev chose to conciliate. 'But *daze* would be good,' she said. She announced that she needed both sex and deep, sensual rest. '*Daze*. Nice word. I could definitely do with some daze.'

Already too much wine; already this melancholy.

Bev would fill Angie in, as much as she could, on the Bloch investigation tomorrow, she added. Not tonight. 'We don't want to destroy the S banquet vibe,' she said, 'with matters non-alliterative.' Angie gave her news. A week after the death of Robbie De Soto, Sam had decided to prolong his leave. There would be no inquest. He was free to disappear. Angie had offered to stay on, to support him, but Sam had another plan. He would spend some time with his brother, his sister-in-law and his nephews, sharing the bedroom of the older boy; then he and Mark would head off on a brotherly trip together, to New Zealand. Angie had listened to this plan with something like disbelief and confessed to Bev that she felt a little rejected. She offered to delay her visit to Broken Hill as long as he felt she was needed, but by the end of his week at home the plan had been settled. It was clear she was not needed.

Robbie's parents sent Sam a card, a thankyou card, full-blown efflorescence, writing that their son had been depressed for a long time, but that he had loved acting and was proud to have been chosen as Hamlet. They added that they were comforted by knowing Robbie was now peacefully at rest in the wide arms of their God. Exclamation mark. It seemed not to have occurred to them that there might be a secular link between the troubled son and the troubled Hamlet, the prince rash, despairing and pathologically curious about the undiscovered country of death. Perhaps nobody but Angie and Sam had made the connection.

Sam pushed away his sense of guilt and wanted to speak of it no more. No one at the school knew what method Robbie had used. There was speculation, of course, but it was another secret, occluded, something held by police and within the

God-loving family. As it should be, Sam said, though he too speculated. Angie fell silent when he mentioned of it. She could not get over the feeling that Sam mourned more for himself than for the boy. And now, she told Bev, he was off on a holiday. New Zealand.

Later, in the car, Bev said, 'Close shave there. We missed a near-death experience.'

'What?'

'Avoiding the seafood basket. Here, over one thousand miles from the sea.'

She was trying, Angie thought. She was trying to return them both to good humour, to give her the captions of a comic response and a relieving tone of mischief.

Bev deposited Angie in the car park of her motel. She drove off into the night, taking her unhappiness with her. Her police accommodation was at another motel. She should not have been driving. They both knew that she should not have been driving. A wave, then Bev was gone.

There was no one about. The street was deserted. The motel, despite its lit sign, looked shut and abandoned. The key, she'd been told, would be left under the mat. Angie left her case in front of the door, number three, and decided on a short walk, to sober up a little and delay entering the room. Outside, the vault of night sky was enormous, the stars extra-visible and bright as the belly of a fish. Free association. The sequined belly of a fish. She lifted her face and the brilliant darkness came to her as a dizzy vision. Not safekeeping, but surplus and a falling upwards. A slim moon ascended, exact and hard, and she rose too, or seemed to, hauled, climbing easy, into streaming light. She could not escape the feeling that the night sky was passing through her.

Angie was still full of the stars, and shiraz, when she reeled into the small room, not sure what scale of image or feeling she belonged in.

And so cold. *Turn on the heat. Go to bed. Recover perspective.*

Heartache, shock, all that flesh is heir to. She was quoting, she was rationalising, she was turning her sky vision into sophistry and drunken embarrassment.

Angie undressed slowly and climbed into the bed. *Consummation*, Hamlet's word. Conclusion. Result. After her inactive day on the train, she had trouble falling asleep. In the all-beige room at the cut-price motel, the prehistoric aircon rattled and sighed, every now and then juddering into boxy life with the flicker of a green button. She wondered how, being so dysfunctional, it continued to reset. Light from the *MOTEL* sign fell in white stripes through the plastic blinds, which did not fully close. This was too filmic to be taken seriously. Something American, nineteen-sixties, requiring only a Cadillac in the car park to reflect *MOTEL* aslant on its bonnet.

And now Angie was missing her husband's body beside

her. The empty side of the bed. On clammy sheets she lay still, recollecting lovemaking with Sam. She was surprised at the vivacity of her sexual memory, how specific it was, and how retroactive. It was a form of beauty, this knowledge, of bodies fitted and confident, of legs overlapping, and the heaving they shared, and of the sweet, ineluctable wellbeing of pleasure. There were times when afterwards they hadn't wanted to fall apart, but stayed locked together, sticky, all sweat, all satisfaction.

In early morning, she stepped outside into blinding light. It was true: the sky was bigger here, above this town in the desert.

Had she been a poet, Angie would have named this particular heaven. She would have tried to get closer by language to the lustrous flush of this dawn. She had expected to feel a measure of radical detachment, but instead experienced a powerful drive to attach, to make sense of the crooked fences, and the long, pocked road, turning at the edges to crimson dust, and the scraggly pepper trees and redgums shaking slightly in a faint breeze, and the squat houses, of wood and stone and corrugated iron, with low prospects and rusty water tanks, and poor excuses for a garden. At a distance lay the anomalous pale green of a traditional park, and she could see how street trees had been lined up and nourished against the general aridity. The whole crouched beneath solar flash and shine, the lit, brittle register of unfamiliar country. What she noticed too was birdcall, and yellow-throated mynas in a high, chiming whistle and, further off, galahs scrabbling madly in a raucous mob.

Two four-wheel drives plunged past, the second slowing to inspect her. A white face appeared, seemed to sneer, then was gone. Wheels on bitumen: the sound of stones and dirt flung up in a vicious spray. In one of the distant houses a baby was screaming; there was an acoustical strangeness here: why did noise travel like this? Was it the physics of open spaces? The metaphysics?

Angie had studied the map at the motel and decided on an early wander to get her bearings. The names of the streets in the centre were all chemical and mineral: Bromide Street, Mica Street, Chloride Street, Sulphide Street. Mercury, Kaolin, Cobalt, Radium: *monomania* was the word that slipped into her head. Everything referenced the periodic table or the domination of ore extraction. It was a tyranny of the inert: machines, wrecks, holes, slag and mullock dumps. She was overthinking, as Sam would have said.

The wide streets stretched towards the alleged centre, where the map indicated the existence of Argent Street. The day was already bright and she knew she would have to return to the motel for her sunscreen. Ahead, looking down the Sulphide Street hill, she could see behind the train station the gigantic black waste heap, and industrial mining shapes and poppet heads, some in use, others defunct.

Angie had barely moved one block, barely had a sense of her own disorientation, when someone loudly hailed her. 'Angie! Hey, Angie!' A voice imperative, and male.

Turning, she saw him: Terry Williams, Tezza, the man whose red Ford Falcon had skidded to a stop before an unknown woman in his headlights. Angie had seen him before she had met him, and now, in a companion vision, here he was returned, doubly real, calling out her name.

'Angie! What the fuck!'

Tezza wore a cowboy hat and a blue-and-white checked shirt and was walking a sour-faced bitsa dog. The dog bore the sign of mauling; like its master, it had only one complete ear. It had a mere stub of tail and streaks of purple, scabby scars, showing like a stain through light tufted fur. Yellow eyes, a low growl. Around its neck hung a spiked collar, which Tezza now and then yanked. Angie intuited danger; such dogs are less companions than objects to inspire fear.

'Yay! Angie! Fancy seeing you here! What the fuck! Hey!'

And then she realised: Tezza must have been returning home when he had almost run down Hannah Bloch on the road. He'd told Angie that he was a part-time labourer, odd-jobbing around small mining sites. But now she realised that he must be based here, in Broken Hill. She'd not wanted his biography. She had dismissed him as incidental. And now he was kneeling beside his dog and giving a human growl—'Grrr!'—as he embraced its head and shook it in a wiggle, roughly loving.

‘Meet Max,’ he said. ‘Say hello to Angie, Max! Grrr!’

Angie was inclined to step backwards. Max stared at her with doleful, jaundiced eyes.

‘Gentle as a kitten,’ Tezza said. ‘C’mon, giv’im a pat.’

And so she did. The dog twisted its fat, scaly head to nudge and lick her hand. A line of shiny drool now connected them. An old dog. Old.

‘There you go. See?’

And it was done. She’d seen his car, she’d met his dog, now they were friends. Tezza and Max walked alongside Angie as he pretended to direct her.

‘Classy part of town here,’ he said. ‘Tourist motels and old pubs. Some of the fancier houses.’ Other than that, he had little to say about his town. He said he worked now and then at the Social Democratic Club, known as the Demo. It had the best schnitzel in town. Thursdays. Thursday-night schnitzel. ‘I can take you, if you like.’

Angie was thinking: *Oh no, Tezza wants a date.*

Together they walked down the hill to Argent Street. Main Street. At this early hour there were no other pedestrians visible: this was a town ruled by cars. The word *classy* belonged in other places; it was amiss here, and inapplicable. The view of the waste heap alone was a disqualification. It was the kind of mass that might exist in the films of Ingmar Bergman—a symbolic black blot, signifying evil or the end of the world. Or Lars von Trier—yes, *Melancholia*.

‘Staying with me aunty, in Uranium Street, just for a

coupla weeks,' Tezza was saying. 'Then I'll head back to the bush.'

Angie resisted the implicit invitation to reveal where she was staying. She considered herself a good judge of character. He was harmless, she decided, even though he looked fearsome.

Tezza touched his hat self-consciously, as men do in American movies, and peeled off to go to the Demo. He was doing some cleaning, the usual bloke, Bill, being off on a sickie. He gave a wave and tugged the surprisingly docile Max. Angie walked in a loop and headed back to her room.

When Bev came to collect her at the motel, Angie could not have said why she didn't mention meeting Tezza that morning.

Transformed from last night's despondency, Bev had recovered her poise and was dominant and sure. They drove in the police vehicle, high and mighty, to the police station. This was not the old-fashioned building Angie had seen on the internet but new, tall and sleek, with an Aboriginal motif mural at the front and a glass and steel entrance.

'Yeah, I know,' said Bev. 'Brand new station. Policing is big in this town.'

Bev gave instructions. 'Keep it vague. Don't say you're freelance. Just say you're "media liaison" and imply that you're linked to police media and have permission to attend. I'll vouch for you if necessary. But don't say you're a consultant or anything that sounds too official. Don't say we're friends. Don't say how long you're staying. Don't answer personal questions. Don't get into any trouble.'

It was an obsession for several years, Bev wanting to play the piano. Between the ages of eight and twelve, she begged her parents with whiny, childish, ratbag desperation to buy her a piano. She would teach herself, she said. How hard could it be? In China, three-year-olds played the piano. And the violin. She'd seen it on telly. There were competitions in which kids no older than she sat rigid in black suits or meringue dresses, layer on layer of white puff, and played Rachmaninoff.

Dad, Senior Constable Calder, raised a comically large eyebrow. *Rachmaninoff?* He reached for his cup and tossed back a mouthful of milky tea like one deeply insulted. Her mother was alarmed, as if her little girl had been possessed by those body snatchers who looked just like real people but were not real people. Gradually they grew accustomed to the pleas but never gave in, never conceded anything so offensive as a daughter who told her parents exactly what she wanted.

Bev described it all, the raised eyebrow, the cup of tea, the mother's panic, the dismissal. 'I am a vanquished soul,' Bev had declared. 'They seek to extinguish me.'

Both girls were alike in this glory of overstatement, in speaking a vocabulary that inflated their feelings. There was a delicious shiver—vanquished, extinguished, Rachmaninoff.

Angie's double ambition to be a train driver and an Egyptologist had been greeted by her mother with polite enthusiasm. Without criticism or expectation, Nora preserved her daughter's ditzy drawings of fabricated hieroglyphs in a folder purchased solely for that loving purpose.

No one was surprised when later, in the city, Bev went off the rails, so to speak, and ended up at the methadone clinic in Chippendale, vomiting into a bucket and crying her eyes out. She stayed with Angie, now a university student, and moped about, raided the fridge, sold her friend's hippie jewellery. In the evenings they watched television or went clubbing together, dancing in the lose-yourself frenzy of an almost ritualistic undoing.

When Bev enrolled to become a policewoman, they were all surprised: her father said he could have been Knocked Down by a Feather. Proud as Punch, he was. Happy as a Pig in Shit. Both parents attended her graduation, the evidence for which was a grimacing photograph slashed by unkind sunlight, so that a squint, shared by all, added the hideous truth that they were still a far from happy family. In her father's slitted eyes shone the pride of forgetfulness; in her mother's some relief that little Bev had turned out normal.

Now Angie was watching Bev perform her authority. No one here knew of her early musical ambitions, or of her wayward snatches of other selves, trying out life. Angie had argued against what she believed was Bev's capitulation, the reactionary choice of giving in to the Law of the Father; in retrospect, her words had been critical and cruel. But Bev found in the police force a role that suited her. Now her voice boomed as she addressed the crowded room in the Broken Hill Police Station.

Some were fresh-faced and appeared no more than twenty; some were older, more senior police, men of a certain age who might have been carved from granite, they were so angular and hard. Cynical, misanthropic, old-school and, like father-in-law Mack, men who boasted of drinking and mistakes in wild and excremental language. Crapulent boasters all. These few men hated Bev, her rank, her confidence, the fact that she stood before them saying that they had to lift their game, reminding them that there had been a terrible crime here, a woman strangled, a baby gone, probably torturous imprisonment for as long as two years. Not the usual break-and-enter and kids stealing cars. Shorty, a tall cop, and one of those chiselled, sniffed loudly and muttered complaints as Bev spoke. Angie looked around. There were also two young women who gazed at Bev in fan-girl adulation. Fifteen men in all, perhaps? The entire crew.

In the end, Bev lied. Outright. She introduced Angie as someone who was working with the public affairs branch of the force, overseeing proactive communication and operational support to investigations through media liaison. She took the words straight from their website. She sounded convincing. And though the staff looked askance at Angie, no one challenged her presence. No one asked for evidence of accreditation.

Angie was learning this new language—how much policing relied on it, how much Bev knew and practised in its dubious regions. Investigations had these dark spots: the unacknowledged advice, the covert whisper, the information grafted, or extorted, or pressured into being. Bev was capable of violence, Angie thought.

Angie stepped outside for a break.

An unknown number lit her phone and she guessed immediately that it was a call from another disappointed claimant. She could have said, *I am not available right now; I am pursuing another angle to my story; can we make another time?* But, hearing an older woman's voice and a tone plaintive and insistent, she agreed to listen to the story and record it for her file.

She had learned to listen. This was her work. First, listen.

The woman was ringing from Fremantle, Western Australia. Her name was Filomena Donato. 'I saw the Germans on television,' she began. 'They didn't seem very happy. If it was my daughter, Cristina, I would have been weeping with joy. I would have fallen to my knees and thanked almighty God.' Her tone was indignant. No forgiveness for emotional restraint and the usurpation of her hope.

Angie had never been to Fremantle, Western Australia. What was there? A port city, large ships, some stacked with sheep for live export. Gentrified buildings from colonial times, warehouses made into restaurants, worker cottages into coffee shops. A shopping mall, perhaps. The Indian Ocean would surely govern all views—a strip of pure shine, a horizon and, closer in, a creased ocean and the gentle rhythm of falling surf. Angie loved port cities; one day she would see the Indian Ocean. One day too, Genoa. And Liverpool. And Buenos Aires. Where had this thought come from? Her longing for other oceans. For ocean.

Filomena was insisting. 'My son Matteo, he was on the web; he saw your number in our support group. I know you are helping to find missing persons,' she said.

Angie's heart sank. Where had this idea come from? How had her modest, implausible project become heroic in this way? She dared not contradict but felt a rising shame. 'I'm just writing a story,' she said. Supplicating. Wanting to be forgiven for all that she could not do. Had never claimed any ability to do. What desperation, to believe someone like her might have an answer.

'So, I want you to add my Cristina to your list. My daughter. She would have been thirty-eight last Thursday. I lit some candles. I said my prayers.'

A silence now, as Filomena gathered herself in, returned to formality.

'The police here have all the details, but you need to know

about Saint Anthony.'

There was a moment of incomprehension. Angie was patient. She glanced at the slagheap in the distance: foul residue, black mass. 'Go on.'

'When I was a girl, back in Italy, living in Pordenone, my mother took me to see the relics of Saint Anthony in the cathedral in Padua. You know Saint Anthony? Patron saint of loss, lost things, lost people. It actually works. You say, "Saint Anthony, Saint Anthony, help me find the car keys," and there they are; they suddenly appear where you had already looked. Works every time. I have told many people about Saint Anthony.'

'And Cristina?'

'I have to wait for Cristina. One day I will know. But let me tell you about the saint. He was famous for his preaching. He had a beautiful voice. He even preached to fishes. This is a well-known story. The saint and the fishes. And when his body was uncovered after his death, his tongue and his voice box were uncorrupted—that's the right word, the priest said it—*uncorrupted*. And "glistening", the priest said, as if used just this morning. So the relics are this flesh inside us that speaks. They were sealed in a reliquary, up high, and when I was a little girl it was hard to see, but I knew the tongue shape was there, and the glisten of life. Nearby was a painting of Saint Anthony preaching to the fishes. I loved that painting.'

Angie waited to hear more of Cristina, the details of her disappearance and the terrible, long wait for news, but

Filomena seemed to be saying she had found consolation.

'Saint Anthony hears my prayers,' she said. 'So if I don't see Cristina in this life, I will see her in the next. And the saint will be there too, with his tongue back in his mouth.'

Angie sighed. Too godless to rejoice, too sceptical to care, she was still oddly moved by Filomena's declaration. This woman saw a saint's tongue as a child and felt not revulsion but validation of her faith. She affirmed voice, and utterance, and stories told by allegory and symbol. She was gullible, needy perhaps, but touched by the luxury of belief.

It occurred to her then that Filomena had no trace of an Italian accent. On the phone her accent was assimilated Australian. What Angie heard sounded archaic, an early piety from another nation, but somehow it had survived migrancy and who-knows-what cultural erosion, to persist as a proud foundational memory.

'And what is it you think I might contribute?'

'Cristina Donato. You must have her on your list. Write it down. Cristina Donato. But please tell everyone the story of Saint Anthony.' A pause. 'There is a saint for everything,' she added. 'Everything.'

Filomena's voice. She had simply rung to instruct. She had rung to check that her daughter's name was again known and recorded, that the investigative avenue was not yet closed—but also affably, to recommend another kind of meaning, to insist on her own vision, the marvellous given recognition in this otherwise disheartening quest. Angie imagined Filomena had retained this scene: the high transept an awed child might stand beneath and stare into, the bank of candles ablaze in their rosy cylinders, the hush of the holy-minded shuffling in an orderly line to stand before flesh, and to marvel. Gilt on marble mouldings scintillant in half-light. Saints gazing down at her.

Angie was faithless. Or lacking a faith that might extend to heaven. Apart from her own mother, she knew hardly anyone who believed in a Supreme Being and Eternal Life. Capital letters.

She moved back into the foyer of the Broken Hill Police Station. It was mostly glass panels, so that the counter was shiny and protected, and there was an intimidating screen, set high, that showed her diagonally and in monochromatic distortion. But there was also a board of pinned notices: the Police and Citizens footy club fixtures, the correct procedures for handling firearms, the new helpline number for victims of domestic violence. At the centre was a large poster of thirty-six missing persons.

Angie counted the faces. Six by six. Thirty-six squares. Each looked stunned, as if caught peering from a window. No miracle of the flesh here, or anywhere, to back them up. And no Hannah Bloch. Had she even been officially noted as missing?

The main team consisted of Jackie, about fifty, a blunt senior constable with bright pink lippy, Senior Sergeant Frank Childers, gruff, bad-tempered, one of the crapulent complainers, and a young woman, Kylie, whom Bev had chosen because she disagreed with something she'd said. ('Independent, a woman not afraid to speak her own mind.') Kylie was a junior constable, not long in the force, and her selection had occasioned gossip.

Then there were the support staff, all fully briefed, and most, it must be said, apparently respectful of Bev. There was a single tech-head, Mikey, and a group of younger men who huddled in a pack, wanting real action, wanting to use their guns, not this boss-femo-nazi act by a blow-in from the big city. Angie heard 'female impersonator', uttered with a slur. She saw and heard everything because they talked as if she wasn't present. All disregarded her, but for Mikey, who slipped her his phone number 'in case she wanted a drink after work some time'. Desperate, she thought, and trying it on. A new woman on the scene.

Otherwise, no one addressed her or sought her opinion, and although a few of the sharper tools in the shed had noticed that she might be a friend of Bev, it was to Kylie they directed their especial venom. There was an Indigenous Liaison Officer, Merle, grey-haired, matronly and self-possessed, but not a single Aboriginal cop on the team. And only two who had grown up in the town, Kylie and Jackie.

On a whiteboard Mikey projected a map already marked

with their search: abandoned mines of the region. In a landscape so flat, the only place for a whitefella to hide was underground, and this was a region with many and various undergrounds: mine tunnels, shafts, carved spaces of hidden life. Angie thought irresistibly of a kind of mythical bondage, the dark labour of gasping and dislocated men, year after year, made red like the earth, hacking away at tough rockface for a seam or a gleam. It scared her, the mining world, with its hard-yakka darkness. She stood with her back to the wall. Clutching her laptop to her chest, scanning the room, Angie realised she was spooked and claustrophobic. She contracted in fear at the thought of an underground.

Then it came to her plainly: it was a mistake to have come to this town and this station. She should have stayed at home, in Sydney, talking to the hopeful and the hopeless and recording the dolorous voices of those who told her, a stranger, that they believed Jane was theirs, and were still undefeated and searching. Like Filomena, most had an unrealistic notion of what she might do for them, as if connection to the world of media, even her loose connection, somehow implied that she might publicise their pain.

Misplaced faith was no better than her own misplacement; this was an unfriendly situation. She had no role here. Bev should not have included her. And the world of crime, she understood, was mostly dull and repellent. For all the deadly fun of plotted drama, this was not her genre. It was not her freelancing remit. She had no wish to contribute to the criminal hunt or its shady forms of titillation.

Once, as a child, Bev held up the putrid carcass of a dead lamb, swinging it like a flag. Its body had been ripped open by a fox and its innards were dangling in a purple mess. Angie recoiled. Bev called her a 'girlie wimp' as she flung the remains in Angie's direction. Perhaps this was so. A girlie wimp. Perhaps ever thus. Perhaps she was more herself away from the challenge of things torn apart.

The carcass returned in nightmares: gristle and bloody remains, sluggish flesh in blobby streamers; a reflex always to step backwards, as though some speck, horribly magnified, might splash crudely and taint her.

Silver, lead and zinc: the largest deposits in the world. All in a lode, all stretching beneath the town and far beyond, out into the desert. Mikey was pointing to mines around the town of Silverton. These were spots on the map with optimistic names: the Bonanza, the Mad Luck, the Lucky Hit. Further north were Tasmania, Germania, Red Lion, Wheel of Fortune, Hen and Chicks, Barrier Chief. All were defunct now except Day Dream, which had been repurposed as a tourist mine; it was excluded from the search.

Kylie, Jackie and Frank stood with Bev, conferring. Circles on the screen indicated which sites had been chosen; some had been searched, and some they might yet search. Interviews had been conducted—everyone in Silverton—but had yielded no useful information. One man dobbed in another as a suspect but this turned out to be the latest chapter in a long-running enmity that included minor theft on both sides and the gruesome killing of each other's dogs.

Lots of tourist visitors, most heading to the *Mad Max 2* museum, but none particularly suspicious, or indeed staying. Nowhere to stay. The five little units at the old pub didn't count. Most came for half a day to pay homage to the movie debris of junky machines, the costumes and masks worn by scary road monsters, and to watch a scratchy video of the hero, standing, legs astride, on a road leading nowhere, or in a scene eating dog food with a fork. (In a glass case lay a handwritten note: 'This is the actual fork used in the scene where Mel Gibson eats dog food.') Thence to purchase a sticker or a fridge magnet, thence to down a glass of beer at the picturesque pub.

Locals had their theories about who had abducted Hannah, some of which were racialised. Bev had read through the transcripts, done some repeat interviews, with Jackie or Kylie taking notes, and decided most were wankers. 'Don't write that down,' Angie was told. Mikey was busy clicking at the keyboard and expanding and contracting circumferences. Both Shorty and Frank said the perp was probably long gone. No point wasting everyone's effing time.

Bev made herself unpopular by saying that the earlier searches had not been systematic or thorough. She was adamant that all the marked sites must be revisited.

Angie tried unobtrusively to work on her laptop but confirmed to everyone in the police station that her status was marginal. Bev had not intended to exclude or humiliate, but the message to others was clear. As Angie was leaving in the afternoon she saw Merle, the Indigenous Liaison Officer, sitting on a spot of patchy grass outside the police station. Before her were two boys, about ten, cross-legged, downcast.

'Hey,' Merle called. 'Join us.'

Angie saw that the boys, in a sense, were in Merle's custody—that she was submitting them to a lecture outside the police station. They were staring into their laps, ashamed, and gave Angie the barest acknowledgement.

'This nice white lady,' she said, 'is visiting all the way from Sydney. You don't want her to think you're no-hopers and crims.' It was clear that Merle had forgotten her name. Or spoke in a pretence of forgetting.

'Angie,' she said. She had never been a nice white lady before, called upon to represent power and severity of judgement. It was unbearable, to be given this role.

'Angie, meet Snoop and Blade.'

Both boys grunted and averted their gazes. One of them, Snoop, was twisting his shirt into a cone. Blade was almost entirely obscured behind the long curtain of his hair.

'Don't worry, she's not a copper. Tell them what you do, Angie.'

And Angie saw then that Merle wished to disperse, or perhaps to increase, her command. 'I write stories,' she said.

This made no impression at all. With rude pity Blade looked at her through his droopy hair. 'For movies?'

'No.'

Merle gave her a glance that said: *You should have lied.*

'Maybe one day.' But no one believed the ingratiating addition.

'Off you go now.' And the boys sprung up, suddenly lively, and fled. 'Just trying to keep them out of the juvie.' Merle pulled a cigarette from somewhere deep in her bra, and a lighter from her pocket, and casually lit up. She inhaled deeply, her head back, her face to the sky. Then she exhaled to the clouds and asked what Sydney was like. 'Seen it on the telly, of course, but I've never been.'

And so Angie began. It had been a strangely wet summer, she said, with the most beautiful storms. The harbour all churning, the bats going wild, the place glossy and alive. She could see that her words meant nothing and that Merle had just been polite. Only when at last she mentioned that she grew up in the bush, in central New South Wales, did Merle show a genuine interest. What town? What family? She had family all over, she said.

And so, by names alone, they began to converge, until at last Merle happened upon one familiar, that recalled a man from the mission. 'You must know Uncle Merv, down that way. Old Wilcannia fellow.'

And yes, Angie remembered an Uncle Merv. An elder when she was a child, so probably gone now. He had lived on the outskirts of town in a shack. He had known her father and she had puzzled over the honorific 'Uncle'. She recalled them together, yarning, as she sat restlessly waiting. Uncle Merv had given her father a dead rabbit, wrapped in bloody newspaper. Her father's hands had the tremors. Discreetly, the old man stilled them between his own, placing the parcel, pressing it there, insisting on the gift. She remembered the stench of the rabbit and her father's bleary gratitude.

Now, telling Merle, this transaction was full of mystery. Perhaps there was a history of friendship there. And Uncle Merv helping her father, feeding their family, showing by generosity his acceptance of the outcast. She had followed her father as he shambled home. She saw that he clutched the bloody parcel as if his life depended on it, as if the warmth there, in that little life gone, was a message for him alone.

Everywhere: the powdery, orange light.

Dust in lurid cumulus billowed behind the car. They were streaking through the desert, jolting on corrugations, fishtailing over sand traps, sparking flint into the sky. A hot wind burned across the spinifex, so that the spiky heads quivered. Spear grass, pigface, minuscule white flowers—all were crushed as they drove.

It was Angie who had rented the Hilux, and Bev, on her day off, was taking control, wanting to gun it like a hoon, she said, away from the cop world of scrutiny, away from her snarky colleagues. She was keen to impress her friend and slightly maddened by her own freedom to lean over the steering wheel and charge at the horizon.

Further out, scared emus, their large eyes alarmed, their movements a sequence of fierce, gangly jerks, bobbled idiotically alongside the car. 'Too stupid to veer,' Bev shouted over the noise of the car. Then at last they did, their fluffy backsides prancing.

No trees at all, but for a single leopardwood and occasional low-slung mulga.

And here was Angie, another white person with a feeling of unbelonging.

In truth, she'd come here for this, to see the desert. For years she'd tucked in her heart the appeal of all that eluded her, the hot breath of this bigger place, the sear of no shade and sunbaked dirt, all she had read of the mystery of interior spaces, how the nation's soul was here somewhere, existing in this colour. It was a kind of desire, promising a verifying force. She had high expectations of sublimity and visions.

She'd looked it up: it was Wilyakali country. Longtime Wilyakali. Now, in the car with Bev, hurtling where she didn't belong, she felt a vague sense of her own intrusion and what might have been shame.

Beyond the windshield loomed the ridges and gullies of the Apollyon Valley. Kangaroos bounced like toys in the far distance, saner, Bev pointed out, and also more curious and trusting. Too easy to shoot. When they were fourteen, Bev's father had taught them both how to use a rifle, and though Angie was the better shot, it was Bev who had taken to it, dispatching wounded animals, popping off crows, pinging just for fun a row of cans set as targets.

When eventually they stopped, they climbed down from the vehicle and stood simply observing. Now both seemed attuned to non-human signs. It was dust settling, the atmosphere correcting itself, the infra-physical hush. Silence resounded for a while, with the wind only visible in its tiny effects, spiralling grains of sand, lifting a few leaf spikes, sweeping gently at always disappearing tracks. April, a bright day, coolish, cold at night.

Bev's voice: 'There: Apollyon Valley.'

There was a rise before them, and the ridges of a formation. And a field of quartz reef, claypans, veins of mica and ironstone: this was the hard world that produced glut and mullock and spall, lead poisoning, fortunes, cave-ins, suffocation. This was the domain of rich-man investors and dirt-poor workers. Angie's sense of rapt entanglement surprised her: to be prone to these images from faded times, to be linked by class memory or sympathy to the tough work-world that had happened here.

She could not resist sharing her knowledge. Apollyon was the devil-beast in *The Pilgrim's Progress*, she said. A mixed-up creature with scales, a lion's mouth and the wings of a dragon. It attacked Christian, the holy pilgrim, on his way to Zion. It was a kind of devil.

Bev agreed that only a miserable bastard, madly disappointed, would name a valley Apollyon. It was a valley of rock.

'He's in this area somewhere,' Angie said. 'He knows his literature.'

And Bev scoffed. 'Clueless,' she sighed. 'It's just a name. Probably from the 1890s. What miner would even know this? And there are hundreds of small shafts here, maybe thousands.'

As if a name might be a guide, this least of our meanings. A name. As if Angie's interest in the arts had any relevance out here. She wanted to say, 'John Bunyan, 1678.' But stayed silent, wisely concealing her pedantry.

Every now and then they came across a hole surrounded by a wire frame. There was sometimes the remains of a windlass, or rusty pieces of old machinery, or a forty-four-gallon drum that might once have held water. And sometimes too there was a modern, painted sign, in sunflower yellow and high-gloss black:

DANGER
KEEP OUT
Abandoned mine workings.
Entering this area may cause serious injury or death.

At the centre of the sign were three cartoons, one a human with a line of erasure across the body, one an image of a rock falling towards the dot of a head; one a figure, a stick figure, stepping into the V of a chasm.

They saw a site from the track and stopped, walked in a circle, appraising, and then stood behind the wire fence.

Together, from the rise of the mullock heap, they stared into the black hole of the shaft.

Bev said: 'Impossible. No one could move a live body down there. And supplies. And whatever. But there are some mines where the entrance is a slope, not vertical. And there are spaces carved out for storage underneath. That's what we're after. That's what we're looking for.'

Angie was inclined to agree. She looked at the abandoned mine, its surface laminated by the sunlight, its dark hole made darker by the angle of shadow, and it seemed to her one more emblem of weary lost hope, of searching in the wrong place. Wealth-sickness and hardship beyond measure existed here.

Here. Old men and young keeling over or crushed underground or dying the slow, degrading death of contaminated lungs. Angie, always imaginative, began to cough.

They passed the turn-off to Purnamoota. Once a mining town, silver mostly, now a ghost town and a cattle station. Angie, wanting to connect, said the name quietly to herself. *Purnamoota*.

And then she said, 'Chromatic.' This was the word for it, the right word, as Filomena would insist, as Alex might ask—not of music but of colour, the way every surface was modified and refracted by this superabundance of light. She thought of it as a quality of intensification.

Bev heard her mumble to herself and turned slyly to see. She offered Angie a smile suggesting—once again—*clueless*. Then she turned onto the sealed road and together they saw roadkill, the dastardly violet smear, chromatically bright, that showed little animals their place.

That afternoon, at a cafe on Argent Street, they met with Kylie. Bev had asked if they might talk informally, away from the police station, and she'd agreed.

Kylie arrived with Jackie, newly lipsticked and almost festive in an emerald-green shirt of impossibly shiny fabric. She plumped herself down with a heavy sigh, as if she'd been jogging. *Theatrical*, thought Angie.

Their secret was that Jackie was Kylie's aunt. They had different surnames and believed no one at the station knew. It gave both of them comfort to behave as colleagues, then to share gossip later on at the Demo or a family barbecue. Jackie was dolled up, she said, in preparation for a drinks date at the Palace Hotel. She leaned forward and whispered, 'A handsome FIFO.'

Angie was the observer; Bev asked Kylie questions with respect. 'Tell us about yourself. And your sense of the case.'

Kylie felt that the measure of her worth was to make herself sound interesting, so had too much to say that was charming or sadly irrelevant. Her netball team, her early difficulties at high school. The death of her father in a mining accident when she was eleven. The dust storm of 2018, when she thought they would all die. Eventually, Bev interrupted to ask again if she had anything to say about the case. Anything they'd not yet talked about.

It was Jackie who answered. 'There's a bloke here, Tezza, odd-job man. You should look more closely at him and his fucked-up family.'

Angie took a deep sip of her coffee. She'd still not told Bev of her encounter with Tezza. Bev waited.

'Known him all my life. His two older brothers were both lead-heads, brain-damaged by exposure. The eldest brother got sick, had convulsions, fell into a coma and died. He'd been working since he was about ten as a sorter and ore-picker. Lots of boys did it. Helping old-timers on small claims. Then mucking around in the dumps. And skidding their bikes. The second brother was a bit slow, with a kind of tremble. He died young too, about twenty. The third went missing—mysterious circumstances. And Tezza, mumma's boy, was kept indoors for protection. His mad mother has a lot to answer for, but at least with Tezza she tried.'

Jackie waited for the women to indicate their interest. 'I'm pissed off, frankly, that Tezza is on the telly, acting like he's a hero. He's a loser, big-time.'

'He was investigated at the beginning,' Bev said calmly, 'when Hannah first turned up. He has a record, stealing cars as a kid, then receiving stolen goods in his early twenties. Seems he was a fence for the odd shovel or bag of cement taken from the larger mines. No jail time, only a fine. A small-time crim.'

‘Still,’ said Jackie. ‘How do we know he didn’t leave Hannah Bloch in the darkness, then return and say that he’d found her.’

‘He was closely questioned. Why would he call an ambulance?’

‘Panicked, that’s why. Not to be trusted.’

‘We’ll look again,’ said Bev.

Kylie, who had been silent, added, ‘I like Tezza. Not a nutjob alpha like some around here.’

Now Jackie was angry. Her lips were pursed. ‘And what would you know, little miss?’

It was a family dispute that lost puff when Jackie decided to leave early. They watched the startling green blouse billow and sink as it receded.

‘There’s a history there. With Tezza.’ Kylie was being disloyal, and knew it, but felt the need to defend her own judgement.

Ah, the joy of country towns. Everyone knows everyone. But the conversation had been enough to make Angie and Bev reconsider.

Kylie repeated for Angie’s benefit what she’d told Bev when she first arrived. In the vast minefields there were vacated places here and there, above ground, sometimes just a wall or two, sometimes a whole structure with shreds of fabric flapping in a glassless window, bottles and rubbish strewn about, or rusty machinery; or car parts, old tools, the ruins of a drum used as a bush stove; or signs of campers taking shelter, or kids building a fire on a dirt floor.

Kylie knew of them but said no: no way could a woman be hidden above ground. She was sure it was a mine cavity they were searching for. If there was a prison, it had to be a mine. Dead cert. And given the remoteness of the location where Hannah was found, it had to be in the area north of Broken Hill. Just not that many people around. Tourists pulling caravans along the sealed road, but off-road, on the dirt, was another matter entirely. It had to be someone local, who knew the place. Someone who stayed put, stayed hidden, while the search continued.

'He wouldn't run,' Kylie said. 'He probably had nowhere to run to. And a local, not a FIFO.' Not one of the new engineer types on the large open-cuts, with high-vis and a credit card, men who turned up at the tourist cafes early morning, spick and span, ready for their cappuccino takeaway.

Kylie's disdain was evident. She lamented the scarcity of good men around the place. FIFOs were just after a quick fuck, she said, and had a wife and kiddies hidden away back home. None of them with enough spunk to capture a woman.

Bev and Angie exchanged glances. There was bitterness here, and inexperience, and disappointment. A young woman wanting out. Kylie's ambition was to be a detective in Sydney.

When Kylie left, Bev told Angie of her fears. Not for the first time, she was realising how she'd relied on Kylie's conviction, how her search had been only for an inconspicuous mine. What if Shorty and Frank were right, and whoever had imprisoned Hannah was canny and long gone? Perhaps Hannah had not escaped. Perhaps she had been dumped at the roadside, then her abductor had driven over the border to South Australia and beyond. A final gesture of guilt or compassion or tidying up the mess. A pang of conscience when it looked like she was close to death.

And there might be more than one man. And there might be a woman. There might be a figure, like a mother, deranged with grief or her own insidious lead poisoning, somehow operating behind the scenes, finding twisted relief in the idea of a woman abused and imprisoned. Helping to drag a weak body through the night to place her there, darkly.

So far, nothing. She'd done no better in locating the scene of the crime than the team before her. There was still no clear suspect.

A shrug. An evasive gaze.

Angie listened. Felt redundant. Wondered if she should wait to break the news that she'd decided to return to Sydney.

IV

On Monday morning Bev went to the station alone, and Angie set off in the rental car to do her own exploring. Rental chariot, more like. She'd never driven this kind of vehicle before—riding high, diesel, four-wheel drive. The road slid beneath her as if she owned it. She sensed how it felt to be a rev-head, or a mechanic, or someone used to off-road adventures and the superpower to roam. She began on the smooth mineral glisten of the newly sealed road and headed north, to Silverton.

Roadkill splatter from the night before—and the wide, open road. She played a song in her head. She'd almost forgotten this roadie pleasure, to be mobile and swift and away from the accretions of the everyday, to be singular, alert, filled with the surround vision she was moving into. The sky arched. The virtual window. The feeling of speedy understanding.

When she'd visited Silverton with Bev, it was Bev's agenda taking the wheel. But now Angie slowed, looked carefully, avoided the star locations of the pub and the corrugated-iron shed that served as the movie museum. The town was a scattering of 1880s buildings, a stone church and a courthouse. A few houses were inhabited, even loved, but they were set far apart, so that the spaces were all defined by what was no longer there. There was not a soul visible on the few orange-dirt streets, or in the paddocks of orange emptiness that stretched between them. Someone, somewhere, was banging metal with a hammer. Reverberative clang travelled far in these empty spaces, just as filaments of white light latticed extra-high in the sky.

But Angie had in mind a destination. The stone jail had been converted to a local museum, its cells and exercise yards filled with an ambition to collect everything. Bev had scoffed and driven past, but Angie arrived at opening time. Old tools, old photographs, old lamps, memorabilia. Cells marked with the faint scratches of suffering now held needlework, dolls in christening gowns and early Edison projectors. Musical instruments, the histories of Scouts and Girl Guides, the Odd Fellows, the Freemasons, the Royal Antediluvian Order of Buffaloes. Every sporting team ever, lined up, unsmiling with tightly crossed arms. Back from the days when people lived here within the pleasure of community. Medals, commemorative mugs, multi-Elizabeths in her crown.

One cell was devoted to mining equipment. Angie bent to examine a gas-detection cage for mice or canaries, and next to it was an oxygen chamber designed to revive gassed birds. A stuffed canary, no longer upright, lay beneath an oxygen tank, its stick legs pointing upwards. Failure to resurrect. Ropes, buckets, mining signs and union banners. Next to the dead canary was a row of carbide lamps and a collection of masks.

Angie stared. What caught her attention was a Fleuss 'self-contained breathing apparatus', a mask that covered the entire face and chest, with tubes like a double proboscis extending from each side of a beak-like nosepiece. The tubes joined more tubes slung across the chest. Angie held up her phone to capture it for storage in what she'd named the Farcical Unconscious, the space where photographic images hid away. It was a trick she practised, to photograph, not avoid, but then to consign the disturbing image to microchipped quarantine.

She was searching for something.

Ever the pedant, she truly loved museums. She had always enjoyed the novelty of earlier lives, how their quaint strangeness unaccountably provoked her. But now the random qualities of objects, of the cute and the ghastly in mind-jumbling miscellany, felt overwhelming.

For the hour she spent in the museum, there was no other visitor. A kind blonde lady of indeterminate age sat beneath a display of rifles in the front room; it was she who had sold her a small cardboard ticket like those once used in cinemas. The woman was pleased to be spoken to. Angie praised the collection but asked about the local Indigenous community and if there were any old maps of the area.

'You missed the Aborigines. The room with the piano. Next to the solitary confinement cell.'

The Indigenous display was negligible. Disgracefully thin. A grinding stone, a woomera, a Namatjira print. Almost no information. The map was in the hallway, a large hand-drawn diagram on paper turned brown with age. It marked the old mines with carefully printed names. Not a single crossing-out. No spelling mistakes. This was the product of a slow, fastidious hand. This was an older map than Mikey's, with a few different names and features. Angie took photographs of each section of the map.

She was asked on departure to sign the visitors' book, in which almost every entry was exclamatory.

Excellent! World class! A fitting tribute to our pioneers!

Angie wrote self-consciously, under the gaze of the ticket woman: 'A mind-jumbling miscellany.'

One day, Angie thought, I will join the world of exclamatory emotion.

It was a swift drive back. In her motel room, Angie transferred the images of the map to her laptop and began to examine them. The mines had fanciful names: Balaclava, Himalaya, Stirling, Beehive, Rupee, Tara, Manchester, Eureka, Dora, Robin Hood, Britannia, Bobby Burns, Florida, Bonnie Dundee, Parnell. Any geomancer would see the pattern there: how foreign stragglers planted their weak hopes in the gesture of a name, how in the land of schist rubble and saltbush, searing and inhospitable, they recited something cherished—a hero, or a lover, or a place half-recollected from a greener world.

And then she saw it—Pilgrim. In the Apollyon Valley,

there was a small holding that someone had named Pilgrim. It might have meant nothing, or it might have meant that a literate miner had known of Bunyan's tale and understood the devilish challenge of the land he found himself in. Angie felt a scholar's thrill of connection, even though it was possibly of her own making. On impulse, she rang the museum.

The blonde lady sitting beneath the rifles immediately picked up. 'Never heard of it. Just a name. Don't put too much store in that map. It's much too old to be of any use. Those mines shut down or were abandoned long ago.'

'But the Apollyon,' Angie insisted. 'John Bunyan.'

'Never heard of him. As I said, it's a pretty old map.' And then there was the sound of a wire door slamming and another voice, moving close. 'Ever heard of the Pilgrim, Harry? One of the old mines?'

'Nah. Only Walter Pilgrim, long dead. And his son, Billy, who lived up at the twelve mile and disappeared a few years back.'

Angie heard it like a gong: Billy Pilgrim. Unsure what it was that had struck her.

She made the effort to sound reasonable. 'Can I please speak to the gentleman beside you?'

'Here, Harry.'

An old man cleared his throat, as if called upon unexpectedly to give a public speech. 'Yes?'

Angie introduced herself as a researcher and asked if she might make a time to talk further. Harry sounded shy—'Not much to say'—but agreed. It had to be tomorrow; he was doing some fixing-up at the museum but would head back to his claim the day after. They could meet at the museum at ten o'clock.

It was, she decided, a quality of nervy excess. Angie could not settle or read or do anything halfway useful. In the airless, drab room of the motel she made herself a cup of tea. An old kettle and two white teacups sat on a bench; teabags and wee plastic containers of long-last milk were available in frugal numbers on a wicker tray. As she shook the paper tube of white sugar, Angie calmed the confusion in her head: motel standardisation had its mollifying benefits, after all.

She untied her sneakers, removed her socks and sat cross-legged on the bed, sipping her tea. And then, feeling the trivial oppression of such a featureless room, wanting to share the story of her day, she rang Bev at the station. Her call went unanswered.

Later Bev texted: 'See you tomorrow night. Too whacked.'

Angie had not yet told her friend she was planning to return home; that could wait. She sensed that Bev had lost confidence and needed to re-establish a boundary, a rank—a structural assertion of her power. It would be a mistake to intrude now. To call again. And there might be nothing significant in the existence of a Pilgrim mine. Yet Angie carried the intuition of having stumbled across a clue to the puzzle.

After only twenty minutes she could bear her room no longer. She decided to walk to the centre again, this time to visit the railway museum on Blende Street.

It ought to have enticed her, but in her current agitation there was something dead and unappealing about stalled railway carriages and walls of redundant metal signs. Only a few people were in the museum. In the outdoor yard of train detritus, a lone boy capered through the empty carriages, whooping and thwacking a stick. Where were his parents?

Angie tried to pay attention to the small objects arrayed in glass cabinets. More collections, more memorabilia. The boy's yell and the bang of his stick persisted. An old man in a railway cap was offended by the ruckus. He left his replica ticket box to holler, but the boy made a point of ignoring him.

Angie couldn't stand it. She fled. She found herself outside, on the street, lost and thirsty. All at once she felt the sweep of an enormous sorrow. Mind-jumbled, yes, still mind-jumbled from the jail museum, but this was also an unexpected subsidence of self. She was recalling photographs.

Garnering objects for museums may have been a struggle against grief. The most far-sighted did not perform for the future. And now the blotched documents of past lives, those photographs of football teams, and workers, and a choir of ladies in puffy hats. All were alive in their own dignity, all with their own inner duration, but had no thought—surely never thought—of being an exhibit. They did not expect the eyes of another era to peer at their faces. How could they imagine they'd be delivered into the world of exclamation?

The thought upset her. Why did she feel so bleak? Everything connected to a disquiet she would later think of as spiritual incompetence.

And Sam. Sam had left her with a brusque kiss and headed off with his luggage; this had seemed like the true intimation of an end. It had been his action, not hers; he had acted to leave. After their years together, there was this dull, perfunctory moment in which she felt above all a disappointment that she'd not been the one to act first. It was a dishonourable feeling that did justice to neither of them. It took no account of the month they had tried, and none of the death of Robbie De Soto and the grave circumstances that had made them, more than usual, strangers to each other. It was so recent a parting but felt long ago, stretched back into a past as remote as the nineteenth century.

As if she'd summoned him by these thoughts, her phone rang and the caller was Sam. She hesitated, resisting the sign of coincidence. Then she pressed the button and said, 'Yes?' as if she had no idea who called.

'Ange, hi. How's it going?'

'Fine.'

'How's Broken Hill?'

What could she say? 'Still figuring it out.'

There was an interval in which the buzz of another country on the phone seemed impossible, counterfactual. But it was everyday ordinary. And in that whole, other country, Sam too was lost for words.

Then: 'How's Bev?'

'She's good. You know Bev.'

It was worse than strangers, this rift, this stilted, empty talk, wary on both sides. Neither could gauge what or how much to say. Angie felt sorry for him. She felt sorry for herself.

'Where are you?' she asked.

'A little place called New Plymouth, on the North Island. Pretty. Quiet. Mark has a friend here. A rugby mate. We're going on a road trip.'

'Great. Look, I can't talk now. Another time, maybe?'

That a phone call across an ocean and half a continent could say so little. That she had so few resources and so little charity to find a conversation. She had already hung up, ashamed of her slack responses and her reluctance to hear him out. Mute and brooding, she stood in full sunlight and thought again about the jail museum, the photographs, the little cages for expiring mice and canaries, the repulsive mask, the man Harry with whom she'd spoken on the phone. Harry was curious, she could tell. He might have been flattered by her request. Again she sought the burden of a practical task and a release from what was personal.

There was Harry, seated beneath the display of rifles, waiting for her to arrive. The ticket woman now had a name: Fiona. She felt it necessary to officiate, as if, having learned that Angie was a 'researcher', she deserved more attention. Fiona was a beneficent presence, superintending. She'd brought with her a tin of sweet biscuits and was offering tea.

This much Angie now knew: take your time. The questions were less important than the trail of a narrative response, what a voice might follow according to the uncertain drives of expression and repression. Angie did not mention the police investigation or her interest in the Unknown Woman who appeared one night on the road. But she did mention missing persons around Broken Hill and watched as they failed to make the connection.

Harry was perhaps eighty, still working as a handyman. He tipped his tea into the saucer, blew on it and drank in one slurp.

'Not too many of my kind left these days,' he said proudly. 'I can do anything. Machines, plastering, carpentry, fixing radios—the old ones, anyway. And mining, of course.'

Angie waited.

'Walter Pilgrim, yeah, he was a character. Mad for the books, he was. A bit of an odd sort.' Harry paused, as if 'odd sort' had been a defamation. 'But kind enough. And good for a shout, even though he was teetotal.' And so he rambled on.

Angie looked at Harry's hands, discoloured, tough as mulga stumps, gnarly and large. He wore overalls splotched with paint, and boots, also splotched, that with the bulbous and cracked quality of age looked much too large.

'Do you know Walter's history?'

'His family came in the boom years from South Australia—Adelaide, maybe. Took up a small claim but never made a go of it. Ended up as a provisioner, taking supplies to miners, water even. Often took his boy with him, after his wife died. He knew the area well, he was reliable. A good sort.'

'And the boy?'

'Billy, yeah, Billy was a bit of a mystery. Did a couple of years at school and then helped his dad. He lived alone in the old place after Walter died and then, about three years ago, four maybe, he just disappeared. Before that I used to see him sometimes in Broken Hill. He was a bit of a God-botherer, if you take my meaning. One day a few blokes in town beat the crap out of him—excuse my French—and it made him even worse, preaching outside their pub, acting like a crank. He gave out little bits of paper with his thoughts written on it. Religious thoughts, mostly. God. Prayers. That kind of stuff. When he disappeared, no one really missed him.'

'When exactly?'

'Three years, like I said. Or maybe two. Not that he'd been very social. He kept to himself, did Billy. But a couple of us heard the shack had no lights on anymore. When we checked, he was just gone.'

Angie waited.

'In a puff of smoke, like.' To add emphasis. No exclamation

marks, just a wish to assert.

'Like a ghost,' said Angie.

'A ghost who walks.' And a smile now, and their complicity, hearing the story they were making together.

Harry agreed to drive Angie to see the old shack. He refused a lift in her vehicle and took control, heading onto the red-dirt road in his battered old ute. It was a rough ride. They were too jolted to talk.

The way seemed long and featureless to Angie but it was only 'twelve mile', and then she saw the wreck of a wood and asbestos shack leaning against a ledge of schist. They pulled up beside it and gazed through the window. This was remarkably like the empty places Kylie had described: a fire had at some stage been made in the centre of the floor, ash blew in light puffs, bits and pieces of a lost life were littered everywhere, as if wind-flung. But she saw it immediately: there was a piano, an old piano, half-shattered and sloping at a precarious angle. She could make out a name—*Broadwood*—in curly gold lettering. Some keys had gone; an absent side panel might have been prised out for a fire.

'Lots of old ones out this way,' Harry said. 'Heaps of us had piano lessons, even the poorest families. Not me. Sausage fingers.' He held out his gnarled hands as evidence.

'No graffiti,' Angie said.

'Not so much. That's more a big-city thing. Broken Hill is all break-and-enter and pinching cars. Poisoning dogs.' Here, a deep sigh; he might have been a dog-owner victim.

They walked around what was left of the Pilgrims' place. Peered in.

'No books?'

'Nah, they would have been burnt. Shortage of fuel, you see. Or maybe one or two taken away. When I broke in with my mate there were a few still here, but I can't see them now.'

Angie would not go inside. She took the opportunity to say she was visiting with the inspector looking into the case of the woman, the Unknown Woman, who arrived from nowhere.

'Not like we took anything,' Harry said, sounding guilty. Now he felt a need to explain or appease. Now she might have destroyed what had been open between them.

Harry drove Angie back to the hire car. He was impressed that a woman would hire such a vehicle. 'Next time you can let me have a go,' he suggested. He gave the driver's door a loud pat as she closed it.

Fiona stood outside the jail. She greeted Harry and waved Angie goodbye. In the rear-view mirror Angie saw that they remained still and speculating, watching her leave.

It was afternoon; she must find some lunch. As she drove into town, Angie saw a police car on Oxide Street. She slowed her vehicle. Two junior constables—one was Chas, one Rick; she was good at names—were inspecting what looked like malicious damage to a liquor store. Each stood with their hands on hips, tough and grouchy. They wore reflective sunglasses and had their thumbs hooked in their belts, as if acting. This was a culture with which Angie felt no connection. But Harry with his sausage fingers, peering at the piano in the ruined house, and Merle, sitting outside with the cross-legged boys, and Kylie wanting out, lamenting the treachery of a FIFO—these workers she felt close to. And Bev. She would always feel close to her darling Bev.

Late afternoon gave the sky a brassy tint. Once again, Bev had not answered her phone and Angie became restless with all that was unresolved. She needed to check on her friend. She needed to tell of her discovery. She wanted to allay her cloudy, possibly invented sense of premonition. Eventually there was a message: Bev would meet her in the evening, after work.

In the motel, Angie lay on her bed and played Bill Evans on her laptop. 'Peace Piece'—free-form jazz piano, recorded during a thunderstorm in 1956. There was the tinkle of Evans' ostinato and the sound of thunder and rain. Angie curled on her side, hearing the notes and weather of another era. Nowadays extraneous sound would be deleted. Such a sentimental thing, rain. Such facile evocation. But it simply entered the performance; it had not been planned, and this old atmospherics, uncontrived, sweetly slow and gently droning, carried her into a state of sleepy calm.

Just to close her eyes. Just to be still. The plastic blinds of the room filtered a soporific light and in its stale glow she shut down, stopped ruminating on museums and the past, dispelled the Pilgrim house with its dead piano and terrible dereliction, submitted again to the lure of rain inside, the self without an umbrella resigned to the immersive and elemental.

Angie opened her eyes to the groggy thought: *And what did he say to Ophelia?*

And the fretful worry returned, that Sam had done more damage, that in his arty enthusiasm he'd not seen what young students might know or think. Even as he conceded his collusion with dark-side excitement and the fantasy of extinction, he had been self-justifying. This was the fun of theatre, he had told her: to exaggerate what scares us, to have a collective of players show the symbolic order and perform the not-said. The lofty aims of art. And the failures of art, she might have added, in the face of youthful complication.

She deleted the thought. Sat up, pulled her laptop close and checked her emails. Sent off a note to her mother about the spectacular desert around Broken Hill. All the emus. The feral goats. When she searched for a photograph to attach, she saw the Fleuss mask again and flicked it away. She settled on a view of the Mundi Mundi Plains, with tiny kangaroos, neat as paper cutouts, just visible in the distance. It was a photograph she might have filched from a tourist site, but it served the familial purpose. *Hello, Mum.*

It was the view everyone photographed from the 'viewing

platform', a car park on the edge of the Silverton Highway. From the windy rise, you could see forever. You could see a memory of a movie. With fast cars. CGI. Hot-shit and dangerous. *Hello, Mum, from here you can see forever.*

There was a knock at the door, and Bev's voice. 'You in there, Ange?' And when she was admitted, Bev began an immediate castigation. 'Why was your phone turned off? Didn't you get my message?'

Angie lifted herself from her slough of despond and apologised for losing track of time. 'Just sleeping.' Her rest had been less a control of all that tumbled than a turning-up of what was stored. Flustered, she looked around for her socks and sneakers. Outside, it was dark and the temperature had plummeted. Outside, the world had turned in space without her noticing.

'Before dinner,' Angie said, 'I have something to show you.'

It was hard to stay focused. How to attach meaning to something obscurely personal and long protected, something she was unable fully to comprehend or describe? The map on her laptop looked amateur and unpersuasive. Bev tilted forward but hardly glanced and was demonstrably incurious. Angie said that parables and symbols appeal to those who need a pattern to make sense. The solemnity of precedent, the intuition of shared meanings. This name, Pilgrim, and this place, Apollyon Valley, were too well matched to suggest coincidence. The family had been drawn here by the promised fulfilment of a name. A dream of meaning.

Bev waved her hand in dismissal. 'Crime isn't like literature. It's not a system of tidy plots and neat correlations. Not like a teledrama, not like a novel. Not,' she added, acidic, 'like X marks the spot.'

Angie waited a beat before saying, 'You don't have too many leads right now. It might be nothing. It might be something. It might at least narrow the compass of the search. This guy Billy Pilgrim disappeared two or three or maybe four years ago.'

'Pretty accurate, then. A disappeared man. A shonky timeline. A fictitious-sounding name.'

'Dinner,' said Angie. They would need another context in which to rehearse their conversation. It was motel living that had worn Bev down, she decided. It was not conducive to reason, this suspension in beige stasis, this inability to prepare one's own meals, this absence of non-utilitarian space and even something as incidental as a small plant or a pretty cushion. There was an initial flush, like a sense of truancy, like forging an escape, but it soon gave way to the commercial tedium of the living space.

Bev agreed. 'Such a drag.' And agreed too that the water here had a metallic taste, that the black dump behind the railway line seemed over time to grow bigger, not recede, that there was a kind of emptiness to the streets, and an inertia that they couldn't quite explain. This they could agree on. What neither mentioned was the look and feel of their own misplacement—the unspeakable sense each felt that their work had lost its way. The fear of futility. And Angie said no more about how she had yielded to a mystery that might, after all, be a rash extrapolation.

They drank too much. Angie complained about Sam, and Bev defended him. Bev complained about Lew, and Angie, who had scarcely known him, mounted a weak defence.

'I behaved badly,' Bev said at last. 'Unforgivable.'

Angie was left to guess what she might have been referring to. 'Constitutional seriousness!' She held up her glass.

And Bev said, 'No. I've had enough.'

Each walked off into the night, to their separate, dreary motels.

Later that night, Angie messaged images of the old map to Mikey to correlate or superimpose, and wrote the location of the Pilgrim house as a starting point. And later still, in a kind of turmoil, she sent the map to Bev. In the morning she waited, and there was no acknowledgement. Such simple technology, a hand-drawn map. In daylight her sense of discovery seemed somehow less plausible, the map less a template of possible meaning. And it may have been, after all, entirely imprecise. It was a scattering of handwritten names on a large sheet of brown paper. It was the combination of Pilgrim and Apollyon. Angie had no way of knowing how accurate the distances and locations might be, or who in their obsession or deviousness had gone to such trouble.

Angie drove to the police station and was met by the tall man, Shorty, who stood in silence at the front desk, towering above her. Bev was off somewhere, he said curtly, off on a wild goose chase. 'Took the cop jeep for an off-road. Her and her sweetheart, Kylie,' he muttered. The resentment in his voice was hard to miss. 'Complete fuck-up,' he added for good measure. His face was all sneer. His chin pointed to the Missing Persons poster. 'Gone missing.' An attempt at wit.

Angie was dismayed. She knew that to do her job Bev must act without her, but she felt disappointed, betrayed even, not to have been told. She walked from the lobby but lingered in front of the station, indecisive, confused, desperate for a cigarette, even though she had given up ten years ago. She consulted her phone again. Nothing. When she looked up Merle was standing before her.

'Anything I can help with, luv?'

And Angie told the whole story. Of her friendship with Bev and the meaning of Apollyon, of her discovery of the map and Harry's uncertain knowledge, of Billy Pilgrim, who vanished and was at least worth a look.

Merle was unfazed. 'Yeh, he disappeared just over two years ago. He was never registered as missing because no one cared. I told Bev this morning when she raised his name. I knew who he was, this Billy Pilgrim. He used to preach outside pubs and drive everyone mad.' After a pause, she said, 'I'm a bit worried about Kylie leading the way. She's keen but doesn't know much about Country.'

Merle lit a cigarette. Angie watched her inhale, silently craving, disgusted at the power of her own appetite. 'They'll kill you.' Trying to sound light-hearted.

'Something will.'

They'd barely spoken to each other since the meeting with Snoop and Blade; now, with courteous restraint, they began re-establishing a kind of intimacy. Merle grew up further south, she said, Menindee way, but north of Broken Hill was her ancestral country. Decades ago her people had been moved from their land to government missions but she was still part of the Wilyakali mob, still connected.

Angie asked her directly. 'Will you show the way? Maybe come with me?'

Merle had seen the impressive hire car. 'Any excuse to get out of the office.'

It was impulsive, possibly foolhardy, but they made a plan. It was Merle who said they should contact Tezza; they might need some muscle. 'He's a good bushman,' she added. 'I know Tezza from way back.'

That she vouched for him meant something. Angie found his number in her phone. Would he come with her and Merle outback, to try to find an old mine?

And he responded with a 'No worries', nonchalant and neutral, as if he'd been asked to pick up milk from a store. He didn't bother with questions but sounded pleased to be included. 'Nothing much going on here in old Uranium Street.'

When she pulled up, Tezza was waiting outside his aunt's house with Max. One hand held Max's collar, the other a rifle, which he raised in a kind of fake-Indian-warrior hello.

'It's okay,' Merle said quietly.

They watched him toss a backpack, a swag and blankets into the tray, and then haul up a heavy plastic drum of water and a box of provisions. He was overprepared, thought Angie. How long had he imagined their excursion? She waited for more loading before she realised Max would travel in the cabin with them.

'Yay!' called Tezza as he pushed Max onto the back seat and lifted to join him.

He peered over the seat as Angie showed the map on her phone. She gave a condensed version of what must have sounded like religious gobbledegook. 'It's a very old book,' she explained, '*The Pilgrim's Progress*.' The story of a righteous man on a journey, a man who sets out from the City of Destruction to travel to the Celestial City. He climbs the Hill of Difficulty, then walks through the Valley of Humiliation, where he encounters the beast Apollyon. The two do mighty battle. Christian is wounded but wins by quoting scripture, and continues on his journey to the Valley of the Shadow of Death. Eventually, yes, he arrives at the Celestial City. There's a travelling companion called Faithful, who is martyred, and Hopeful, who takes his place.

She had the strong impression that Merle and Tezza were bored. But then she reopened the map, stretched and moved the images, zoomed in, zoomed out. These names, these locations had an antique glow, the folds of old age, the inky quality of hand script, the ragged, human tilt of names inscribed, not printed. Small details of gradient were cross-hatched, and a few natural signposts indicated. They were peering into a past.

Angie saw the cartographical intelligence there, and something else, inaccessible to most, remote as the ultrasonics of bat migrations or the pulse of particles invisible to the naked eye. She felt as she had the first night she arrived here: a kind of desert thrum behind everything, a pressing-in of mystery, a shift in the dimensions of what one might know. Ignorant of the local, she had seen the belly of a fish in an ocean of heaven, and she had felt an unaccustomed, woozy swoon. It was too located in blood beat to dismiss as delusion, or disorientation, or inability to deal with scale.

She read the mine names aloud. Their anomaly struck her again. A Bonnie Dundee in the desert. A Florida. A Parnell.

Merle gestured to take the phone. Held it up, and closer. This was her jurisdiction. 'I know this area,' she said in a whisper.

Tezza now realised they were looking for a cop. And seeking a man who might be connected to the appearance of the woman he still called Jane. In the drama of his small life, she was his moment of distinction. The TV cameras. His face elsewhere. People stopping him on Argent Street, like he was famous.

He too had seen Billy Pilgrim preaching outside pubs.

'Not Billy? Nah. I felt sorry for him. A nutter and lonely. You got the wrong man there.' Still, he wanted to come. He wanted another adventure. 'Not Billy,' he repeated.

Angie and Merle said nothing. How had Tezza and Billy known each other? Police work, even this pretend kind, required perpetual suspicion, and now Tezza was again a figure of suspicion, lodged in who-knows-what undisclosed relations.

They were driving north-west. They headed again along Silverton Road, and at some point would pass the turn-off to Day Dream, then move off-road towards the Pilgrim shack, then to the Apollyon Valley, and further, onto what Angie thought of as the pilgrim trail. She considered their position on a map of Australia and couldn't imagine location, only direction. North-north-west, near the border. Then turn east.

And so again she was tearing through to a bigger space, an outer world that stretched further than she had ever seen before. Racing into the map in her head and the novelty names and the confusing effect of their outlander disconnect. When they turned onto the dirt track, Angie was forced to slow. She discovered the driving was more difficult and the way more treacherous.

Max leaned his head towards Angie's face and seemed keenly to enjoy the ride. He panted hard at the jolts and swerves, his ruddy tongue lolling. This too distracted her, this doggy life looking on, this fat-headed animal, all puckered muzzle, watching and drooling and apparently deep in concentrated thought. She wondered if the clinging odour was as strong to her companions.

Merle and Tezza had begun to speak to each other. Both were bird-spotters, it seemed. They named birds ejected in a blur from spinifex and bushes, or whizzed skywards in the barest glimpse above: yellow-throated myna, crested pigeon, then a black-shouldered kite, slow by comparison, and high, swooping arcwise on air currents. 'There,' they said, 'there.' And Angie slowed almost to a stop, so she could watch the cruise and the elevation and the symbolic reminder to observe. In this almost treeless scrubland, in this whitish light, she had been blinkered before, seeing only large creatures. Merle and Tezza were excited by the small and the less visible.

After a couple of hours, they stopped for a breather. With dog joy and a sniff of freedom, Max charged off into the scrub. Tezza took a piss. Merle found her cigarettes. The sky was brighter than smashed glass.

It was late afternoon before the stark landforms, rising and jagged, indicated they had come into the centre of the valley. There were acacia trees, gullies, ledges of quartz. And as they drove along on the bush track, which sometimes disappeared, they saw on both sides, now and then, signals of human activity: leftover bits of machinery, wired-off shaft holes, danger signs, most amateur and older than the ones she'd seen with Bev. A hand-painted sign read *Danger, stay away!* and depicted a skull and crossbones. A couple of shafts had a few planks simply dropped across them as a cover. There was no indication that any of the mines were still used or that there had been any recent activity.

'My mob's Country,' Merle said sadly. 'My grandmother brought me here as a child.'

They edged along the dirt road, jerking at the rough, sliding sideways in the soft. Merle saw it first and called out. It was the police jeep, half-hidden and on a rise in the distance. Angie pulled to a stop.

And now the sky flared, rose-pink and golden. Tezza became anxious. The sun would set, he said, at five forty-six exactly and they needed to make a camp before the dark. They had walked up to the jeep and found it empty, but to set off now to find the women would be a risky proposition, especially with the shaft holes and no sense of which direction they had taken.

Angie consulted the map. Pilgrim was an area, not a precise location. This was the correct mine cluster, but the group of names might cover a kilometre or two; there might yet be an arduous trek to come. For all she knew, they had moved into a world of error; she must trust Merle and Tezza; she must stay calm. Angie looked up at the sky. More airy fire, and a pattern of folds and streaks. There was no phone reception. Bev would have used an iridium satellite phone to tell her colleagues of her location and intention; if anything went wrong, support would surely arrive in the morning.

Tezza was beside her saying, 'Best not to shoot a roo or a goat. We shouldn't let anyone know we're here. Not just yet. Not till we know what's what.' He had brought curry powder, he added, in case a nice goat came their way. But was issuing a warning.

Bush cunning, preparation, a worry that he might have to feed them all. Angie let him take over. Tezza prepared a fire in a hollow, so that it would not be visible, and set about boiling water for tea.

Angie was afraid of the rifle. She wished he hadn't brought it along.

From his box Tezza magicked a loaf of sliced bread and a dozen eggs. A pan, spoons, but only one tin mug. Blankets smelling of dog.

And so they huddled, passing between them a single tin mug of tea.

'Do you think Bev and Kylie are in trouble?' Angie asked.

'Nah, prob'ly just settled down by their own fire for the night. Having their own tea. Like us.'

Only later Angie realised this was a kindness Tezza had concocted. To reassure them all in the uncertain darkness.

The world resolved to this: a contracted and provisional safety, a small fire in a wilderness of broken and raided earth, a dwindling glow in the west followed by the wave-sweep of darkness. Angie felt bare and unaccommodated, alive in a quiet way, aware of her own body as heavy. Each stared at the fire. They ate their bread and eggs. Slowly the stars flared and moved them deep into the night.

'I can tell you the story of this place,' said Merle, 'but only our section of the story. Wilyakali part. The story starts with Adnyamathanha mob, over in South Australia, and moves here, then further away towards Tibooburra, and right up to Queensland.'

Angie and Tezza remained silent, their faces down.

'So there was a bird, bronze-wing pigeon, we call it Marnpi.'

Angie looked up; Merle was staring at Tezza.

'And back in Adnyamathanha Country, out near Waukaringa, a boy tried to catch Marnpi with a net. The boy wounded Marnpi and it flew here and sat down three times at the Pinnacles, ten kays south of Broken Hill. You can still see the shape it made in Country. Three peaks from where Marnpi rested. Then he flew and sat on Broken Hill, and he left the shapes of himself there too. Some have been mined away, some of Marnpi's signs, some signs of his body. Each time he stopped to rest, he formed the land.'

Merle paused. 'It's not just shapes. Marnpi dropped feathers, which became gold, silver, copper and lead. You can see the colours. You can see the colours on his wings. And the quartz is the fluid, leaking from his wound. You can see it in the ore, the colours of Marnpi, and you can see bloody rocks, and the silver, and the shine of his leaking life. All those colours in what whitefellas call gneiss and schist. And you can follow the trail of his flight by our story or by the sites of the mining towns. Many towns are gone now. Ghost towns all over. But it was Marnpi left those minerals. It was Marnpi made this land.'

Tezza raised his head. He was moved; the women could see. A wind had sprung up. They listened. Drew the blankets closer. The fire began sending up showers of thin, sparky light.

'Your turn,' said Merle.

And it was Tezza who spoke. 'I don't have nothing pretty like that. No story that makes sense. No bird. My whole life is a complete fuck-up. Done nothing, seen nothing, was a disappointment to me mum. Me three brothers all dead, and then Mum, from the cancer, eating her gizzards out on the veranda because she wouldn't go to the hospital. "Wouldn't be seen dead there," she used to say.' A grim smile. 'But then, fuck me, there was that woman, Jane. I was driving along, minding me own business, and there she was on the road, and I saw her in the headlights and I stopped and I saved her.'

It was not a boast; it was Tezza's announcement of a purpose and a role.

'I know I wasn't the only one,' he went on. 'But I knew it, that a real thing was happening to me. I'd had these heavy dreams, dark stuff I can't talk about, but then, after Jane, I had a dream of seeing a woman in a beam of light. It happened again and again, her returning to me, real late, in the dark. Shining, I'd say. Jane returned to me shining.'

A long silence. Tezza was snuffling, wiping his nose with his sleeve. Beside him, Max raised a fluffy eyebrow, concerned. Tezza, wobbly, embarrassed, grabbed his dog's head and shook it. 'Grrr!'

Merle had been listening with an air of encouragement. 'Well done,' she said. 'That's a good story, Tezza. Proper good.'

Her turn. Angie said, 'I don't really have much of a story.' She saw their glowing, expectant faces, and tried, though self-conscious, to find something to contribute.

'When I was a girl,' she began, 'I was interested in ancient Egypt. We lived in a small country town and the thought of this other place far away, another world, another hemisphere, seemed to complicate what I knew. They had three hundred and sixty-five days, like us, but three seasons, Planting, Harvesting and Inundation, when the Nile rose and flourished. I loved this idea, a season of inundation. There were years of drought in those days and the farmers spoke of rain as a dream. They gazed into dried-up creek beds and held back their tears.'

Angie had seen her father return home coated in dust, and it was dust they all feared, the land gone dead and the sense of it blowing away. Her father had been working on dams, working on hope. But the work was diminishing. The hope was diminishing. He had come home with sweat trails the only moisture to be seen, and him downcast like the others, and defeated by the dry. No work. No pride. And farmers everywhere in despair, and skinflint, and fast going under.

And her father, another named Billy, had shot himself with a rifle. Bushman way, against a tree, holding the gun with his feet.

She was used to managing this secret and would not expose it now. She knew how to turn the lock. She knew how to go quiet. But her voice was unsteady. Her voice by firelight was quavering.

'The birds,' she said, moving away from what was private, 'the birds important in ancient Egypt were ibis, sacred ibis. They were a lot like the ibis you see in Australia. But in Egypt they were revered and stood for a god called Thoth. He was depicted in temples in human form but with the head of an ibis. He was the god of wisdom and writing.'

She sounded thin, teacherly.

'Ibis, yeah, I've seen them,' said Tezza. 'Real mongrel birds, eh?' In his voice she heard not disparagement but curiosity.

'They were mummified in their millions, killed, gutted and embalmed. They were folded, their long bills were tucked beneath their tail feathers and made into a neat package. Placed in urns and underground caverns. Millions.' She paused. 'They were farmed to be sacrificed.'

'Fucking hell.' Tezza leaned forward and, to do something, added sticks to their fire.

Angie was unsure now how much more she should say, aware her story did not sound personal, nor of this place, nor meaningful right now. She was controlling her helpless anguish to explain something inexplicable to herself. The propitiatory gesture. Her emotional idiocy in thinking for a lifetime of dead birds, instead of her father. All the energy of her talk was directed by restraint.

'Afterlife,' she said cautiously. 'The Egyptians believed they were preparing the birds for an afterlife.'

And that was it. Her throat had closed. Her impulse was to talk about the soul being weighed against a feather but she could not have said why. She could not inflect this story with all that it meant to her. She could not account for her attachment to a storybook from her childhood, nor say aloud that she had no belief at all, did not believe in an afterlife, or in myths, or in the revival of the fallen world.

She had caught the train west as the planet moved east, and now she was thinking of south and north, and of time, and of ancient Egypt, and of the fact that the story of Marnpi dropping feathers must have preceded the mines that erased some of the remembered landforms it created. And that the story itself was likely older than the great pyramid of Giza.

Merle had fallen asleep and was curled against the cold, her brow furrowed. Tezza was still awake, staring into the fire, drinking his fourth mug of tea.

At last, he lay down in the tray of the car. His head rested like a lover on his dog's ample stomach. He had ceded his swag to 'the girls', so Merle and Angie, sharing the gift, held their bodies together under the wide-splayed, drifting stars.

In first light she saw what they had missed the day before, a drawing in the sand, an ibis head—clearly an ibis—framed in a kind of cartouche. It was on the far side of the car; she saw too how they had missed it.

Beside the ibis was an arrow, pointing east. This was Bev's little joke, guessing she might follow. This was Bev saying, *Look, it's juvenile, all this bird stuff.* Not detective intelligence, but a childish game.

Yet Angie thought the image oddly prescient and wondered how accurate the direction might be. Had they done a reconnoitre, seen something, then headed back to show the way before investigating? Or had they simply set off due east?

Like her, Merle and Tezza both woke with the sunrise. Tezza was squatting at the fire, stirring a billy of tea with a stick. He yawned, sniffed under his arms and scratched his broad chest. They ate slabs of bread stuffed with tinned sardines. Tezza tipped sardine oil into Max's begging mouth. Then Max flashed away. They watched as he ran circles, sniffed, perked up, turned again and bounded back with a smile.

Merle lit a cigarette. That craving again, the body taking over. She winked at Angie. Gestured good morning with a tilt of her ciggie. Wood smoke, cigarette smoke, the lungs taking it all in. Tezza wore a different face this morning, eager and boyish. Merle was serious, inward.

And then they began. With Max now on a rope, Tezza and Merle led the way, tracking eastwards, warily alert, moving with careful tread and on the lookout for signs. Merle was muttering softly to herself. Tezza was preoccupied. Max strained at his tether, nose downwards, insulted to be tied. Whether this was searching or madness, whether their traipse together was muddled intention or necessary logic, or a kind of narrative desire born of a drawing in the dirt, Angie did not know. She followed with quiet, trustful steps.

The gravel crunched and slid beneath their feet. Shaft holes and mining rubbish showed where the earth had been invaded. And on the surface, a shuddering, as the low wind moved.

It was close after all. There was no time to feel any fear or thrill. Merle pointed at a tiny spool of smoke unwinding. 'There.'

The shaft entrance was mostly covered by a rusty panel of corrugated iron, but it was set into a mullock mound, and possibly hid a slope, not a vertical drop.

They crossed a small gully, careful on the rise, and were approaching at distance when a man appeared. He stepped from behind the iron panel and held up a rifle.

'That's Billy,' said Tezza. Max growled.

Average height (why had Angie expected tall?), wiry, his limbs tough-corded beneath shorts and the shreds of an old plaid shirt. Billy had a prophet's beard and a bushie's squint. He planted his feet squarely. 'God bless,' he shouted. 'Now leave.'

Tezza was transfixed. He made a show of handing his rifle to Angie, then raised his arms slowly, like one surrendering in a movie. 'Billy, it's me, Tezza!' And he advanced with Max, still growling, so that Billy could see who he was, could recall their connection and the world of mates and the time they had been outsiders together. 'Tezza!' he called again, like a man unsure of his own name.

Billy nodded. 'Now leave.'

There was a distended moment, vacant and strange, in which they stared at each other. A crow cawed above and they both looked up. A ruffle in the air that might have been wing-beat. Then Tezza made a mistake. He let go of Max's rope, believing perhaps that Max, in his munificence of love, would revive the feelings between them, that no one could resist a slobby dog, running fast in greeting.

Billy steadied his rifle and fired. Max spun backwards with a high scream and rolled across the dirt. And now Tezza was screaming too, and running, and now the crack sounded again and Tezza was shot in the guts. He grabbed himself, astonished, folded at the knees and flopped forward. No fury visible in Billy, only this stiff resolve to kill whatever came near.

Merle and Angie were silent. Leaf skitter and low wind. Something shifting gear. Angie raised Tezza's rifle and stood her ground, carefully aiming. Billy raised his rifle. And there were two cracks in the air and it was Billy who fell.

Oh, the world turning faster and the blood of a man from a rifle shot, Tezza who hurt no one but loved his dog and was in the dirt face down and the world turning faster still and no directions and no meaning and Merle sprinting to Tezza, flinging, turning him to the light, taking his head in her hands and moaning and he was blinking half-gone, holding on, his cheek twitching, and Merle touching his face and wiping, uselessly wiping, trying to wipe it all away.

They had driven hours over rough country and come to this.

Angie dropped the rifle. Stood for a moment, stunned. Then she moved to inspect Billy, to confront the body, to see what another death looked like. She did not bend down. She nudged his side with her foot. She avoided looking at the face but saw the beard, wiry and streaked with grey. Disgrace: there was an element of disgrace in her manner.

Behind, Merle wailed in a low, faltering voice.

And then, as if compelled, Angie turned to the hole of darkness and stepped inside.

It was terror she felt. Billy was gone and Tezza lay dying, but she stood, adjusting to the dark, rigid with a more indefinable fear. The shaft declined before her. Nothing. A ledge to nothing. Gradually, she understood there must be a source of light ahead, because the timbers and walls of the shaft came implicitly into being; what enclosed and contained her manifested in the barest indication.

She moved with one hand sliding along the jagged rock wall and the other stretched trembling in front, like a blind woman, apprehending. Beneath her feet were flints and the shards of earliest labour, and all around a murky stink: old meat, shit and blood. She might crumble now, into the dust she trod and the bones she imagined underfoot. Without her own source of light she could only move towards the glow.

She assembled enough of herself to think a complete sentence. *What if I can't get out?* The gradient and loose stones made her feet unsteady. A closeness in the air, a humidity and then a strike—she bashed her head. When instinctively she touched the wound it was wet, bleeding. She had sense left to crouch and continue her way bent humble. She would not defer, or turn back. Feeble now, her face sticky, her own wet making a trail in the dust. And she had another thought, one her mother would have considered blasphemous: that she could lie down here in the tunnel of black, give in to her own wound and, in mothering darkness, simply die.

A human sound roused her. A word, or two. The tender tone of something whispered seemed to pour into space. She listened carefully. Nothing further. And began again, still cautious, still muzzy, holding her arm outstretched before her to meet the unseen.

It emerged like a vision, held in a cave of yellow light.

The hewn space, the scripture painted on canvas banners, the single kerosene lamp that was the sole, modest source of illumination. A goat, its entrails stuffed in a metal bucket, hung cut open and stretched beneath the twenty-third psalm. And there in the shadows, a wire cage, crude and dingy, and in the cage three women.

Bev lifted her chin in a wordless hello. She was wounded, her left shoulder a shawl of black blood. Kylie was with her, cradling. 'Is he gone?' Kylie called.

Angie said, 'Yes, he is gone.'

And then Kylie cried.

The third woman was unknown—another Unknown Woman. All skin and bone. She stared at Angie disbelieving, with wide, afraid eyes. Angie knew then that she too had become a vision, come sliding from the darkness, and inexplicable. Like Hannah in the headlights, Angie emerged, to their amazement, a break in the order of things with advent and impossible interruption.

She did not want to look around her. She did not want to take it in. She turned to the women in the cage and focused there, on the human. Tried not to retch.

And then, just as quickly, she thought nothing of herself. She knew only that she had to act to release the women. She scrabbled in a rush, and then she saw it—a junky pile of old tools. Her hands plunged in, rummaged, pulled out this and that. Hammer, saw, a tin of rusty nails. And then wire-cutters, and she heard herself say aloud, 'Wire-cutters.' Her own hands and their competence. Her own two hands.

Her fingers ached as she worked. She saw the pincers and heard the snap and had a sense of her own labour, wire by stiff wire. The shush of the women against her own heavy breathing, caesura, urgency, and then the measureless opening up.

How would they move? Angie ripped down the psalm and spread it flat. The unknown woman showed the learned reticence of her suffering: she cowered, held back, made herself smaller. But consented at last to be touched and then lifted, with Kylie's help, onto the canvas sheet. Angie bunched the end, tugged, and began to drag her out first, holding the lamp. Bev would be heavy; she would need to return. Kylie decided to stay with Bev.

'I'll be back, I promise.'

It pained her to leave the others in the darkness; she sensed their fear.

The way was slow and she hit her dumb head a second time. The surface she dragged the woman over was all impediments, spall and snags. More than once, she sank to her knees, shaking and tearful. And then light, and more light, and by her small steps they were there.

Angie left the Unknown Woman at the mine entrance so she could accustom her eyes to the outside. More stickiness, leaving her own scarlet evidence, and then Merle was there, rushing towards her, stained herself, from Tezza. Merle saw the blood and the Unknown Woman and covered her mouth with her hand.

'Come,' Angie said.

Now they entered together, Merle holding tight to the hem of her shirt. Back on the slope, and crouched, this time pushing away the darkness with the lamp's seeing arc. Kylie was unhurt and had been trying without success to carry Bev. Angie and Merle heaved and supported their hurt friend together. Kylie moved first now, leading with the kerosene lamp. The slope again. Its difficulty. All of them moving bent over. And whatever abomination that was, whatever was there, closing in a slow, twisting aperture behind them.

In the light they were united, hypothetically, provisionally, at least for the time being. Five women in the pact of sunshine and the sweet breeze of a rising day.

Slow with the slog of dragging the canvas sling, they headed back to the cars. Angie could barely stand now but found a power in her limbs to lean forward, to pull the human load, to place one foot after another. Merle and Kylie were holding up Bev, who suffered with her own effort. The bodies of the men and dog were left behind, where they had fallen.

Hand-painted, cursive script. Angie saw on the canvas:

shall not want
still waters
righteousness
shadow

She hated this stuff. Tears of blood. Candlewax.

The unknown woman had turned her face to *the shadow of death* and her breathing was shallow, her eyes were closed. It was still too bright, or she might have entered a private dream of resurrection. In any case, Angie had pulled her from a grave. Her skin was greenish decay, chapped and scabby. There were lumps of sores on her stick-thin arms and legs. Her face needed its privacy.

They rested in a time both expanded and compacted.

They knew only that it was a long wait by the police jeep until the others arrived. Then they saw rancorous Frank Childers dissolve into gentle care; he tended the woman on the ground before he became brusque and bossy; held her head gently and dripped water into her parched mouth, practised his first aid, dabbed at her sores, covered her with a blanket. Before Bev, he was silent and deferential. He examined her wound and pronounced it ugly, clearly impressed she'd barely flinched as he pulled back the cloth. Bev's mouth was slack but she managed a joke; she told Frank that he was a fine nurse and he responded, 'Too right!'

If they communicated distress to each other, it was with the sincerity of small actions, and in each action a quiet, inner reckoning no one could yet name or speak.

Merle and Angie requested cigarettes and a constable sprang forward to oblige. Angie's head was spinning from her wound. She may have tipped over or lost her own being in time, because she came to in the police vehicle, with the constable, Rick, driving a rough path. The unknown woman was in her hire car, held by Kylie, driven by Merle, and Bev was with Frank, slumped beside him in the jeep.

Angie felt—what?—devout. These people were dear to her. She felt her own heart and her shallow breathing and looked across at Rick clutching the wheel, and she thought how young he now looked, and how awful his haircut was, and how his knuckles were those of a small boy, clutching a toy. Her head felt inflated, and still damp, even though Frank had wrapped it in something clean. Outside, brightness at noon, and grainy light, and a clean glow ahead. And all became the motion of the drive, the rock and the jolt.

In convoy the three vehicles sent up clouds of orange dust. How had they looked, she wondered later, this anxious, rushing caravan of the law and the wounded, for which a point of view from the sky showed the discrepancy of human scale? The dead and the saved. The rushing away. In the scrub, on the plain, they might have resembled a procession, something ancient or mythical, plunging through the dust to a promise of safety.

Before they left, Frank inspected Tezza and Billy and declared they were not going anywhere fast. He would return with forensics from Sydney to search the mine.

Another constable, Chas, pleased to see some action, was left to guard the site and watch over the bodies of the men. He said later that it was the dog he really felt sorry for. 'Poor fucking dog. Who fucking shoots a dog?'

V

Then Angie remembered.

In the Broken Hill hospital, patched and medicated, she sought the Unknown Woman. A solicitous nurse led the way, and said, 'Only five minutes.'

The police guard repeated, 'Five.'

At first Angie merely sat. It was a pale blue room, smelling sharply of hospital. The blinds were down, so she waited in an aura of drowsy brown light. Spindly bushes outside cast quivering shadows, seeming to funnel a kind of nervousness, seeming to make the look of things unclear.

The face on the pillow was closed. It bore a remote, absent aspect, consigned to medicinal otherworld. Angie waited. But soon enough, worried by the ticking away of her few minutes, she touched the woman's hand and her eyes slowly opened.

'You're safe now,' Angie said. 'You're out.'

The woman closed her eyes again and Angie felt defeated. It occurred to her that perhaps this woman was also unable to speak. Then, still with closed eyes, the woman whispered, 'Did Hannah make it?'

'Yes, Hannah is safe. Hannah is with her family.'

And now the woman opened her eyes, studied Angie's face for confirmation and began silently to weep.

The nurse appeared at the doorway and Angie made a hand signal: *Five more minutes, please.*

She waited. She stared at the emaciated face struggling with revival. At last she asked, 'Are you Em? Do you have a sister in Queensland called Lisa?'

There was such a loud sob that the nurse rushed in. 'Enough—see how you've upset her?'

But Em said, 'Let her stay.'

And there they were, the bandaged stranger and the half-dead woman given back her name. Angie embarked on a ramble, constructing a connection for both of them. She did not ask questions. She did not speak of the cage in the mine. She riffed tentative and slow on what little she knew.

'Fiji,' she began. 'Lisa told me you sold your car for a trip to Fiji.'

Em looked up at her in disbelief, then in belief. She was confused and teary, permitted now to feel something other than fear. Her mouth was open, her stare was fixed, and she watched the face that had spoken her name.

Angie did all the talking. Words spilled out easily, like a kind of love. They might have been old friends. They might have been dreaming together of a holiday jaunt, or a generic beach in splendid Fiji.

For a short time, all that had befallen them receded. Words did this, made the only restoration they could rely on. Both hurt, Em grievously, and both wanting the threads of spoken sentences to deliver them to a safe elsewhere. In whatever transition it was, feeling held them together.

After their conversation, Angie phoned Lisa from the hospital. There was silence at first. Then she heard the gasp, the surprise and the noisy relief. All around, hospital life remained orderly and sedate. Someone pushed a rumbling trolley along a distant corridor.

Oh, Em. Oh, Lisa.

It was a bleak time, afterwards.

The next day, Angie was discharged, her bandage conspicuous, when hers by comparison was so small a wound.

She wandered the streets of Broken Hill alone, doing her best to cover the sign of her injury with a sunhat.

It was not that she did not see it. She saw the evidence of a kind country town, mothers meeting with their prams, children shuffling in lines into their classrooms, old folk sitting quietly, in veranda shade, turning pages of the newspaper. Shopkeepers made small talk in chirruping tones. She received sympathetic glances, and an elderly lady, concerned, asked if she'd been in the wars. When she ordered coffee, the tattooed barista, in braces and shirtsleeves, stared at her, deeply interested.

But this was a zone of slow time-wasting, checking her phone, dragging herself along Argent Street, lingering over sugary snacks. And everywhere she heard the voices of crows. Her writing too: rough squawking. She hated her writing. No more journalism. She had no wish to continue in the hollow inside her, the inarticulate embarrassment at her own starring role, her now garbled emotions, stretched like a carcass, her inability to adjust to her part in the killing and the saving.

Angie visited Tezza's aunt Flo, but was not allowed beyond the front door. Flo stood behind the flyscreen, darkened and blurred, full of simmering misery and accusation. She believed that the foreign woman on the road was an ill omen of some kind. She had guessed that disaster was coming. 'Complete disaster.' Tezza was not in his right mind. Stranger than usual. 'And you, you fucking police.' Spat out like a spear. Before Angie could respond, Flo slammed the door.

Angie was interviewed by police staff, bigwigs from Sydney, and offered counselling, which she refused. Her presence at the shaft would not be mentioned in public reports; it reflected badly on the force, she was told, to have civilian input. She agreed. It reflected badly. To have civilian input.

This time, she was told, news would be carefully controlled. There would be a coroner's inquest, sometime in the next few months, but a suppression order would keep Angie's role and identity secret. Deception was implied: a story—why not?—that Bev had shot Billy. With Merle's and Kylie's cooperation, Angie could be expunged from the event. A gruff voice, a man leaning forward, his thick arms on the desk. 'Like you were never there. Smoke and mirrors. Nothing more to bother about.' Then he added, 'Just a thought.'

And she saw that he was remembering the constables, perhaps, or wondering about Bev's cooperation, or calculating whether he'd said too much on the topic of deception.

It took three days to arrange Bev's transfer to a hospital in Sydney; Angie organised the remaining time around her visits. Em had already been moved and was now protected by the police and disallowed visits from strangers.

So they spoke, she and Bev. So they waited together. Bev was tired of being brave, or perhaps plain tired. Her face had lost its defiance. It was difficult to assess the change effected, but cheeky bravado no longer worked. She sounded like one trying and failing to disown the ravage of her own thoughts, and her wound, and all that she had seen.

'Can't read. Can't listen to music. Tell me a story,' said Bev.

There were too many to tell. In the past, she had told Bev the plots of novels, or movies. Cautiously, now, Angie retold Tezza's story, subdued and in memoriam, to give him some honour. It was an eloquent version in which his numinous encounter carried no suggestion of omen or violence.

Bev looked at her sceptically, as if she were a fool. This was of no interest, a fuckwit chancer seeing visions, sticking his nose in. A man not to be trusted. How could she and Merle have been so stupid as to invite him along? 'Tell me another one.'

And then she told Bev of Saint Anthony, who preached to fishes and could be relied upon to help you locate your lost car keys. The name: Filomena Donato, seeking Cristina. No tongue yet; she would save that detail until Bev was healed. Make it into a joke.

'Enough already.' Implacable now, Bev asked for a movie story.

Angie began as irrelevantly as possible, choosing, since it sprang to mind, *Elevator to the Gallows*. Nineteen fifty-eight. Directed by Louis Malle, starring Jeanne Moreau.

'Noir,' said Angie. 'Miles David soundtrack. It opens with Jeanne Moreau, tearful, whispering in tight close-up, "*Je t'aime. Je t'aime.*"'

Now Bev was interested.

'She is Florence, her lover is Julien, former parachutist in the French Foreign Legion. Together they plot to murder Florence's husband.'

Bev was listening intently. Angie struggled to remember the names of the characters but managed to convey the contorted story: the plot gone wrong, Julien stuck overnight in an elevator, Florence believing that he has deserted her. All romantic mischance but nothing too grimy or unsolved. It is mostly raining, and Jeanne Moreau wanders the city at night, seeking her lover. Angie tried to convey the glamour of Florence's desperation, her face wet with rain, filmed under neon, converted by movie magic to sheening black and white.

So there she was, Angie sitting on a plastic chair in the Broken Hill Hospital, solemnly entertaining. She was recomposing a hospital room into the screen memory of a movie, so that in binding wakefulness they shared the amusement of old-time crimes of love.

When she asked Bev what had happened to her, her friend said, 'Later, in Sydney.'

Angie knew only that Kylie could have run away but had stayed at Bev's side; that she had pressed on Bev's shattered scapula and staunched the wound; that she had been taken into the cage when she might have been free.

In Sydney, the gust of her own ghost sped by. She could not relax her vigilance.

Sam, still abroad, was not informed. Angie wanted the time alone; she wanted to be in her own place, with the fig trees and inclement nights and the chance to gather in slow motion her centrifuged self. Outside, blown rain, and the world shivering and shapeless, the streets awash, and chill, and though she tried prudent habits—a walk by the bay, reading the papers, a trip to the shops—she felt only a magnification of her sense of being lost. She wept at small provocations and was emotionally erratic.

She might rejoice to have found Em, but her solitude

was invaded. There were phantoms and presences. There was Tezza, hanging around, not resting in peace with his three brothers but in some drastic limbo, forever chasing an out-of-control Max. And Bev, subdued and depressed, and now subject to police discipline. Bev's wound would take months to heal and her sick leave had been extended. She faced demotion, or even expulsion from the force, being unable to explain why she had let her friend, a journalist, into a police investigation. Bev rang to express her wretchedness and her new-grown anxieties. Her voice was different now, vaguely imploring, clearing her throat as though upset, like an old man, Angie thought, like an old man at the bus stop whose sore body and irritation took this rough, grumbling form.

And Billy. Who she had killed. Who she could have shot in the leg but went straight for the heart. She had wanted to kill him. Something had arisen in her that was murderous. And all that blood. His was a pool, shining with light, and her own face was a mess with all that leaked and smeared from the gash on her forehead. She'd caught sight of her frightful self in the side mirror of the jeep and saw there, in glassy blazon, what she had become.

Merle was mourning Tezza and had gone to her own mob for a while. She rang and texted Angie, all of her messages kind, but was distant and strained. Kylie too was on leave. They'd exchanged numbers but neither had rung.

In this time of interregnum, of readjustment, Angie dreamed of them all, and of the cave in the mine, at which repeated occurrence she always awoke, her small heart banging. It was of course nonsense to imagine herself a ghost, but she could not quite recover faith in her own materiality, which now recalled physical heft and open wounds and the bodies of Hannah, Bev and Em. And, more than that, of her own capacity to kill. Easier to absent herself by some spell of willed alienation.

No one yet knew exactly what Billy Pilgrim had done, or how he had captured and entrapped the two women in the mine. If he was a silently wrathful member of some misbegotten group, or if, puny and baleful and shrill with a desire for control, he had made his own vicious laws of deviation. The scripture on the wall seemed to Angie the cliché of fictional crime—a religious madman unhinged, a wish to claim textual authority, the predictable trope of biblical lines transmuted to an evil scrawl. In TV versions there was often a close-up, a shocked reaction to muck and grime, and then a detective bravely stepping forward to a low, jangling soundtrack. She resented the formula.

And still the mystery of Billy. Motive seemed a radically inapplicable word. And no trace of a baby had been found. When they'd met in the hospital, Em said that Hannah gave birth soon after she herself had been taken, and that she had acted as midwife to a baby girl. Both had seen the infant as a sign and thought that Billy might change, or relent, or even release them. Then the baby disappeared. And then they lost hope. Lost hope in signs.

And now, by all accounts, Em was silent too, wanting to say no more. Not yet. Em was inaccessible and needed time. Too difficult to speak of it, too entirely violating. She would only speak, in confidence, to her sister Lisa.

On another planet Billy had once been a little boy playing or listening to a Broadwood piano. He had been earnest and pious; he had helped his widowed father; he had read books and studied beyond the circle of their hut on the saltbush plains at Silverton. But it was a bitter cause he had found, and a cruelly practised power. The piano no longer upright. The sound of it gone. The growth of ferocious intention. The girl that Bev was, too, all those years ago, before police work and her own invidious despair. Bev, who had seemed all her life unhappy, and wanting a system to fit into, a pattern of action and a role to play.

No goodness and mercy following the days of their lives.

One night after her return, Angie woke not by nightmare or storm but to the soft patter of rain. It drew her to rise and pull on her dressing gown to check the windows. But there was no bluster, and the bedroom was peaceful and enclosed. Curiously, she was unalarmed by this incomplete, domestic dark. She did not switch on the light but felt her way downstairs, then groped by instinct, listening for sounds in the house. A dog bark seeped from outside, dampened and afar; the hum of the rain carried a tone of pacification. Downstairs, by a faint glow, she slid her hand along the wall and guided herself towards the kitchen, where she would make a cup of tea.

Rain-light streaked the glass in its own silver shine, and with the curtains drawn open there was the small courtyard, transformed, and beyond that the trees, shrubs and houses of the bigger world. Beside her now, familiar furniture was reduced to black forms, and there too, in the sitting room, with its lines of bookshelves and two old-fashioned standing lamps, her own contingency asserted itself and she saw her own masking within the night. It was a sweet obliteration. The border of her skin was gone. She felt connected to the dark. There was some sense that she might merge hereabouts, and disappear.

And this too: the realisation that the house and the city were now littered with remembrances of her marriage. There was the glint of a lamp visible, somewhere in a far house, and now she trained herself on its small, lit sign, and with this oblique, mysterious prompt she thought of Venice again, and how she had walked into churches full of souls while Sam waited outside, and all about were faces, ancient in candle-light, with luminous, heavenward eyes, and the varnish of ages on old names, and the smell of damp wool and sweat, and no clear language at all but vesper-whispers that seemed to rise up and encircle her—and then too, his sullen stare when she emerged blinking, stunned, not sure where she was, her senses distracted, uttering something vague about the weight of feathers.

It took a moment before Angie realised that there was no wind. The rain was steady because the wind had at last subsided. And that she was only half-awake. Or half-asleep.

She was still jetlagged and now experiencing a second autumn, only colder.

It was with some trepidation that Angie approached the apartment block in Berlin. It was not in upmarket Wilmersdorf but in the poor end of Kreuzberg, and now, with the shadowy season, it looked forbidding and dark. Wild-style graffiti in lime green covered the bottom of the building and flourished like alien rash across the heavy grey door. There were Ukrainian flags draped in windows, and a poster for hot yoga. A small Asian food store, shabby and half-wrecked, was closed down nearby. Leaves in the gutter and her own spirits failing and falling. A man sped past on a bicycle that pulled a cosy pod of two small children, rugged like stuffed toys. Sky the colour of ash.

The names on the door were from everywhere: Russian names and Ukrainian, Israeli and Arabic, two from China and Türkiye, one possibly Norwegian. Among the German names she saw it: *Bloch, Rachel.* Angie pressed the buzzer and the heavy front door clicked open.

On the fourth floor she arrived puffing and found the door had been left ajar.

Rachel was inside her tiny kitchen, brewing a pot of coffee. 'Come in and sit down,' she called.

When Rachel entered the front room with the steaming coffee and two mugs, she was remarkably like Hannah: mid-thirties, serious, with a scholar's grave beauty. The room was furnished simply: a Bauhaus poster, framed, a sofa with three cushions, neat bookshelves and a comfy chair, over which leaned the tulip head of a reading lamp. Rachel gestured that Angie should sit beside her on the sofa, just far enough apart.

Such a stillness here—no volatile air, no sounds but the barest hint of muffled voices arising like smoke from the street.

So what did they share?

Rachel said a little of her family, and of her grandmother, Else Ausländer. Both Else's sisters had died in the war, and she and Esther had been given their names.

'Esther?'

'Hannah. Hannah always hated being named after a dead sister—she thought it was morbid, fateful somehow. Felt that it doomed us both. So at fifteen she took a new name. She named herself after Arendt, Hannah Arendt, her heroine. Always wilful, Hannah, and much bolder than me. We didn't really get on, but I loved her hugely. Still do, of course. Love her.' A long pause. 'She still hasn't spoken. Nothing. Nothing at all.'

Angie waited for more, but Rachel was turned away, seeming to watch something afloat in the pallid light beyond the high window. 'Tell me,' she said at last, 'about this place, this Broken Hill. Why is the hill broken?'

'Named by a German,' said Angie.

'Yes?'

'Charles Rasp, who discovered the silver, made a fortune and named the town. An Englishman, I'd always assumed, but he was born and raised in Stuttgart and studied in Hamburg. He was named Hieronymous Salvator Lopez von Pereira.' Angie paused for effect. Such an impressive name.

Rachel continued gazing out of the window, detached.

'In the eighteen-sixties he moved to Australia, hoping to cure his bad lungs. He ended up in the driest parts, working as a boundary rider on sheep stations. After silver finds nearby, at a place called Silverton, he was on the lookout for wealth, for silver. The story goes that he saw a land formation that he described simply as a broken hill. But it was there, more wealth than anyone could imagine.'

'Broken,' Rachel repeated. And now turned to look at her.

Angie heard the banality of it, the lack of imagination. 'To the Indigenous locals it's not broken at all, but the mark of a wounded bird coming to rest and leaving its impression in the earth.'

'Ah.'

'And leaving the minerals there, too, as it bled and shed its feathers.'

Rachel was distracted again. Angie had given too much information.

'And you?' Rachel asked.

'I was just visiting. I was writing something on missing persons.'

And so they began slowly to meet each other, to discover what Hannah still meant to them, and how the parents were coping, and what it might be like for her, this Esther-Hannah, living in care.

It was almost an hour before Rachel finally asked. 'They said there was a baby. Do you know anything about a baby?'

'Only that she is now among those listed as missing. But Hannah was not alone. Another woman, Emily, was with her, and she helped with the birth. Saw your niece emerging. Helped, was there.' Angie saw how important this information was. 'So Hannah was not alone,' she repeated.

'Another woman?' Still incredulous. Or realising with horror that her sister's tragedy was double. '*Eine zweiter?*'

Rachel rose abruptly to show that this was enough for now. She stood for a moment with her left hand raised to her face, in the turned-away pose of one who has forgotten something important. Revelation of the second woman had not been easeful or palliative. There was a tense, brittle wait in which neither knew how to act. Then Rachel moved close to Angie and both hesitated before the hug. They embraced with the relief of it, this circle, this coming together.

The Spree was a shimmery mirror as Angie left the Ägyptisches Museum and Papyrus-stammlung. She walked slowly across the bridge from Museum Island. Friedrichsbrücke: she was still learning the names in the city. Heading for Hackescher Markt S-Bahn. And for the liveliness of a crowd. And for the noise, and the voices.

And coffee—she wanted coffee.

She had not yet put away childish things. She had sought out the Thoth artifacts and stared expecting something that did not happen. What had she expected? To feel her past self, odd and dreamy, reconstructed? To confirm here that there was no harm in these early attachments, that it was a searching for right images, and a right weight, and a right proportion to things? How a soul might be balanced by a single feather? But still she felt guilty. She had a choice, after all, and had aimed for the heart.

And she had leaned her face close to the glass and seen him there, the 'god without a mother' born from the lips of Ra at the very beginning of time. As the ibis he laid an egg, which contained the world. He invented writing. He witnessed the weighing of souls. He bore the head of a bird. How she had loved him, her child love-object, her wish for a figure far away to display in a system of images all that couldn't be named or spoken. Even Bev, piano-fixated, had liked the exotic story of Thoth.

She would ring Bev and encourage her to come to Berlin. They could talk this through. They could console each other.

Now she was crying once more and not sure why. She was Niobe, all tears. *Hamlet* again. Mourning. *And what did he say to Ophelia?* She couldn't ask him. Sam. Would never now ask Sam what he had said to Ophelia.

Below her, the Spree seemed not to flow. She gazed at the surface, saw the consecutive ripples at the edges, and the nervy, metallic shine. In this pattern the wickedness of the world somehow retreated. She might find consequence here. She might stay, for the time being.

Who said that? *For the time being.*

It was her mother, after the event. They were both still in shock. 'We won't think about him, your dad, for the time being. We won't speak of him at all. For the time being.'

And so she moved forward, across the water, and back to the throng of the streets. The path ahead was beginning to fill with pedestrians of many nations. She looked at the sky, silver-grey—too early for snow—but was already existing in a kind of blue, her mind alive with jitter and riff. She decided to return to her room and listen to jazz.

Miles Davis, the long track entitled 'Shhh/Peaceful'.

The trumpet with its own voice. Saying 'time'. Saying 'being'.

Acknowledgments

This novel was written on the land of the Gadigal people of the Eora nation. I pay my respects to custodians past, present and emerging.

I also acknowledge with gratitude the Wilyakali people on whose lands this narrative is partially set. This novel includes the story of Marnpi, the creator bird of Wilyakali lore. I initially came across the story in a native-title submission and thank the traditional custodians for kind permission to mention it in my work. I thank in particular Sandra Clark, of the Wilyakali Aboriginal Corporation, and her family, as well as the Broken Hill Local Aboriginal Land Council. The Wilyakali were granted native title to their land in August 2023, after a fifteen-year struggle instigated by elder Maureen O'Donnell, who passed away in 2022. Glen O'Donnell and Dulcie O'Donnell were also part of this struggle.

Written sources include John M. McDonald's 'Restorative Justice Process in Case Law' *Alternative Law Journal* Vol. 33, 1, 2008 and the article 'Wilyakali and archeologists collaborating to map the journey of the Bronzewing Pigeon, Broken Hill, Western New South Wales, Australia' by Sarah Martin, Dan Witter, Dulcie O'Donnell, Raymond O'Donnell, Sandra Clark, Raymond O'Donnell Jnr and Badger Bates, *Archeology in Oceania*, Special Issue: Negotiated Narratives of the Past, Vol. 59, 1, 2024. Badger Bates is a proud Barkandji artist who has depicted Marnpi in his own work. Amanda Stone of the Broken Hill Local Aboriginal Land Council and and Councillor Ross Hampton at the NSW Aboriginal Land Council have also been warmly helpful. I acknowledge with deep gratitude the generosity, patience and resiliance of Sandra and the Wilyakali community in both sharing and keeping their culture safe.

Thanks: especially to Kyra Giorgi, for close reading, wise advice and ever-precious support. And to Victoria Burrows for her devoted bird-knowledge and astutely intelligent advice. To Conny Lösch for the initial *krimi* challenge and discusion; Marion M. Campbell for her virtuosic writing and jazzy conversation during my work on this book; Don Mee Choi and Jay Weaver for gifting me a calm space in Berlin to edit; Hilary Fraser for exemplary hospitality in London; Emily Booth for the seafood basket (to a soundtrack of Bryan Ferry); Wenona Byrne, for the handy Broken Hill article; and dear friends Debra Adelaide, Mireille Juchau and Susan Midalia; also Meg Brayshaw, David Malouf and Brigid Rooney.

Sincere thanks to Michael Heyward and all at Text for their consistent support; to Jane Novak, ever-staunch, and not least, Julian Welch, for incisive and timely editorial advice.

'Her own beliefs did not stretch as far as heaven' is a slight rewording of a line from John Burnside's poem 'Responses to Augustine of Hippo. Part 3: De libero arbitrio' ('and lacking a faith/that might extend to heaven'). Sadly, John died during the writing of this book.

The dance scene derives from Lavinia Greenlaw's 'So within, she forgets herself as seen./She is pure direction, she is line and ring' in 'The Silent Disco' from *The Casual Perfect*, Faber and Faber, 2011.

'The monkey and the plywood violin' are cited in Leonard Cohen's 'First We Take Manhattan', to which Bev is referring. It was recorded by Cohen for his *I'm Your Man* album released in 1988.

The wave-poem analogy is from 'To the Reader' by Denise Levertov, *The Collected Poems of Denise Levertov*, New Directions, 2024.

A few lines from Geoffrey Hill's poem 'On Reading Crowds and Power', have been in mind during the composition of this book: 'Quotidian nature ours for the time being/I do not know/How we should be absolved or what is fate.'

Also, Robert Lowell's 'Pigeons (For Hannah Arendt)' after Rilke's '*Taube, die draußen blieb*'.

The epigraph is from Louise Gluck's 'October', *Averno*, Farrar, Straus and Giroux, 2006.

I acknowledge the Media Unit, Public Affairs Branch, NSW Police for advice.